Born in Edinburgh in 1906, **John Innes Mackintosh Stewart** was educated at Oriel College, Oxford, where he was presented with the Matthew Arnold Memorial Prize and named a Bishop Frazer's scholar. After graduation he went to Vienna to study Freudian psychoanalysis for a year.

His first book, an edition of Florio's translation of *Montaigne*, got him a lectureship at the University of Leeds. In later years he taught at the universities of Adelaide, Belfast and Oxford.

Under his pseudonym, Michael Innes, he wrote a highly successful series of mystery stories. His most famous character is John Appleby, who inspired a penchant for donnish detective fiction that lasts to this day. His other well-known character is Honeybath, the painter and rather reluctant detective, who first appeared in *The Mysterious Commission*, in 1975.

Stewart's last novel, *Appleby and the Ospreys*, appeared in 1986. He died aged eighty-eight.

D1232350

Michael Innes

THE MYSTERIOUS COMMISSION

HOUSE OF
STRATUS

This edition published in 2001 by House of Stratus, an imprint of House of Stratus Ltd, Thirsk Industrial Park, York Road, Thirsk, North Yorkshire, YO7 3BX, UK.

www.houseofstratus.com

Typeset by House of Stratus, printed and bound by Short Run Press Limited.

A catalogue record for this book is available from the British Library and the Library of Congress.

ISBN 1-84232-746-1

PART ONE

PORTRAIT OF AN UNKNOWN GENTLEMAN

1

Charles Honeybath stood in his big north window and surveyed the London street. There was much in the scene which might have been expected to interest him. The plane-trees over the way were intricately peeled and pied. The pavement they shaded was still faintly moist from a recent shower, and here and there an oblique sunlight struck from its surface a glint as from some scattering of microscopic gems. A side-street coming in slantwise on the left recalled, through some mere accident of relative heights in its receding façades, one of those exquisitely sophisticated trick perspectives which it had once amused Andrea Palladio to build into the celebrated theatre in his native Vicenza. Odd things happened to the apparent stature of humans, or bulk of buses, as these perambulated or lumbered towards or away from Honeybath's well-appointed studio. Even in their familiarity as a daily spectacle, these appearances might have been expected, we repeat, to bring a glint of absorbed attention to the painter's eye.

But Honeybath's gaze was dull. 'Lacklustre' would perhaps have been the word chosen to describe it by an observer of somewhat literary inclination. Honeybath was a portrait-painter, and it was a long time since he had been anything else. If he had done quite well – and scores of boardrooms in the City of London, dozens of senatorial chambers in provincial universities, even numerous dining-halls amid the superior sanctities of Cambridge and Oxford, attested the fact that he had so done – the achievement had been at the cost of a high degree of professional concentration within this

3

comparatively narrow, if interesting, department of artistic achievement. Until people had faces – and few of those in the street before him appeared to run quite to that – they didn't much interest Honeybath. A psychologist, indeed, might have been able to devise amusing experiments proving that Honeybath had simply ceased to see faceless people. He was a devoted man.

At the moment (as for several weeks past) no object of this devotion was in sight. Trade was slack. This is something which may at any time befall even the eminent. What Honeybath read about in his newspaper as the stagnant state of the economy was no doubt the cause. Prosperous as he had been for a long time, it yet mightn't be long (he was positively coming to feel) before he began to experience the proverbial emptiness, or at least lightness, of the artist's purse. He had several times of late thought of sending out for one tiresome model or another, and adding to the world's existing treasury of art a beggar or a chef or an acrobat or a Chelsea Pensioner. But who would put up any money for *that*? Speculative labours were always disheartening. Honeybath was glum.

An unremarkable if prosperous-looking car was coming down the street. It passed the bakery invisible on Honeybath's left. It slowed before the bank next door. It swerved towards the kerb and drew to a halt – yes, drew to a halt – before what was undoubtedly Honeybath's own front door. A faint expectancy, almost certain to be cheated, came into the painter's eye.

The car was chauffeur-driven – which was a promising detail. The chauffeur got out, opened a door for his passenger, and removed his peaked cap. This was more promising still. Honeybath surveyed with a sharpened attention the emerging object of such deference. He tried to make out whether the man had a face, bone structure, a skull, even just a complexion in which the slightest promise lurked. But the only judgement to come to him was that the man had something faintly wrong about him. This was disconcerting, and the more so because the effect was not readily analysable. Was there a minute discrepancy between the man's clothes and something else about him? Honeybath didn't know. And as for a face – well, the chap seemed notably unprovided with anything of the sort. 'Nondescript' would be the right word for him. There was even a suggestion – despite the car and the chauffeur – of something indeterminate about his social class. Not that his social class mattered a damn – Honeybath with a sudden robustness told himself – if he wanted to have his portrait painted and was prepared to pay up.

And now the doorbell rang. Charles Honeybath braced himself. At least he had a caller. There could be no doubt about that.

'The name is Peach,' the caller said.

Honeybath made a courteous gesture towards a chair, but he wasn't favourably impressed. English idiom forbids a member of the polite classes to say 'The name is Peach'. 'My name is Peach' – yes. 'The name is Peach' – no. And Peach is an absurd name, anyway. It holds incongruous associations. A girl may be a peach – or could be one when Honeybath was young. But a man can only be a peach (it is to be supposed) if he peaches, and at Honeybath's public school you had peached if you told tales. Honeybath began to look for something underhand in his visitor.

'May I ask,' he said smoothly, 'to whom I am indebted for the introduction?'

'It is entirely a matter of your reputation, Mr Honeybath. I must apologize if I have breached professional etiquette in any way. It must be my excuse that we have been advised on all hands that it is to you that we should apply.'

'Not at all,' Honeybath said – vaguely but now rather graciously. He was both puzzled and mollified. He was puzzled because this competence in address was somehow unexpected in Peach, and mollified by the civility of the expressions offered him. He had marked, moreover, that significant 'we'. Peach was some sort of confidential person, he decided, who had been sent to negotiate on behalf of some other person or persons. He was a clever clerk who had got as far as being secretary to some substantial company, and his directors had despatched him to open talks about a possible portrait of their managing director or their chairman. And they had provided him, for better effect, with one of the company's cars. Feeling that he was now seized of the situation, Honeybath accompanied his expression of civility with a cordial bow. 'May I offer you a glass of sherry?' he asked. 'It seems a reasonable hour for something of the sort.'

'I don't mind if I do.' Mr Peach (although back with another wholly inadmissible locution) made a small gesture which was entirely a gentleman's. He might have been taking a correspondence course in the techniques of social elevation, Honeybath thought, and have got to about Lesson Six. The effect was amusing rather than offensive, Honeybath further thought, to one who, like himself, wasn't in the least a snob. But what was it all in aid of? Honeybath poured his second-best sherry, and waited.

'May I ask for a start,' Peach said, 'what they work out at?'

'I beg your pardon?'

'Your usual line in that sort of thing.' Peach was glancing easily round the walls of the studio, upon which several oil portraits happened at the time to hang. 'Would twelve hundred guineas be near the mark?'

Honeybath was startled. He was startled both by the unusual baldness of this inquiry and by the fact that twelve hundred guineas *was* near the mark: it had indeed been his precise figure for several years. He began to suspect that Peach, despite his intermittently odd manner, had been pretty well briefed about what to go for.

'Well, no – I'm afraid not.' It was much to his own surprise that Honeybath – at present unemployed as we have seen him to be – heard himself produce this reply. 'Two thousand guineas is at present my fee for a portrait, Mr Peach. Unless, of course, some special circumstance or connexion suggests the propriety of a different figure.'

'Thank you.' Peach, who didn't seem at all disconcerted, accompanied his words with a small bow suggesting that propriety was quite his thing too. They were back, so to speak, with Lesson Six again. 'And may I ask,' he continued, 'if that includes hands?'

'Certainly.' Honeybath was impressed. Hands are usually an extra, and work out at a hundred guineas each. So here was further evidence that the fellow had been taught his onions. Behind Peach was somebody who knew his way around. And anybody who knew *that* would also know that two thousand guineas was a pretty stiff demand from Charles Honeybath. It was this thought that had thus prompted him to declare that he himself was in the generous habit of throwing in eight fingers and two thumbs gratis. 'But robes, orders or decorations,' he hastened to add urbanely, 'are another matter. They can be very tricky, my dear sir. Particularly when they clash with the flesh tones. So anything of that kind has to be a matter of separate negotiation.'

'There wouldn't *be* anything of that kind.' Peach appeared quite clear about this. 'But I am instructed to say that, in general, any little pecuniary difficulty that turned up would be settled entirely at your discretion.'

Honeybath began to feel that the situation sounded rather promising. At the same time, there remained something about Mr Peach that prompted caution. It was true that the early stages of arranging a portrait commission were sometimes oblique and even mysterious. For example, in both commercial and academic life the proposal to present a notability with his likeness can be pretty well a matter of handing him – as in *Treasure Island* – the Black Spot, and it may seem desirable that the plan should be far advanced before a breath of it reaches the chap who is thus to be railroaded out. It was a shade unusual, however, or so Honeybath thought, for *pourparlers* to be opened through a person of Mr Peach's sort. In any case, it would be sound policy not to give the impression of jumping at what this clerkly person had been deputed to bring along.

'Of course I shall be delighted,' Honeybath said, 'to discuss any proposal you have to make, and equally delighted to give you any disinterested advice or information you may seek. Frankly, it may turn out that you would do better to go to another man. For a portrait, Mr Peach, cannot be executed satisfactorily except upon the basis of an established personal relationship. And that can be – can it not? – a hit-or-miss affair. For this reason it is customary – on the whole, and if painter and sitter are not already friends or at least acquaintances – to arrange some informal meeting before any agreement is entered upon. And again, one likes to know a good deal more about one's subject than the address of his tailor and the shape of his nose.' Honeybath as he said this produced a well-practised whimsical smile. 'One likes to read what one can about him. And even to pick up a little in the way of anecdote and gossip from his connexions – although in a discreet fashion, I need hardly add.'

'Nothing of the kind would be possible in the present case.' Peach finished his sherry, and glanced at Honeybath sharply and confidently, as if he had sensed that two thousand guineas was going to prove a potent bait. 'In fact your sitter,' he continued, 'would be anonymous. I am instructed to refer to him as Mr X.'

If Charles Honeybath wasn't exactly staggered by this bizarre information, the reason was an almost fortuitous one. Not long before, he had heard from a fellow portrait-painter about something of just this kind happening. His colleague had been offered a really large sum of money – much more than was on the carpet now – to execute, under conditions of the utmost secrecy, the portrait of what proved to be an African gentleman of the most marked sophistication and intelligence. He had, it was clear, emerged from an emergent country, whether constitutionally or otherwise, as its President, Prime Minister, or Top Man. And while in London he had wanted a slap-up portrait of himself (which was a blameless and indeed honourable ambition) with no publicity and no cheques passing. This recollection now gave Honeybath pause. The flesh tones customary on the Niger, the Congo, or the Limpopo are undoubtedly very tricky indeed, and such as require much study in an artist accustomed to paint pallid provision-merchants, or pale-pink décolletée dowagers, or the refined but rosy progeny of the proprietary classes for the walls of the Royal Academy in Burlington House. Robes, orders or decorations are child's play in the

8

comparison. If this was the state of the case, the price could be pushed up quite a lot.

'May I ask,' he said, 'whether your client is black?' Having produced this question, Honeybath was conscious that it might have sounded a disparaging and even racialist note. 'Of course black is beautiful,' he added hastily. 'Veronese is only one of those who did amazing things with negroes. And Carpaccio sometimes, too.'

'A black?' It was apparent that Mr Peach was uninterested in these aesthetic reflections. There was even a hint of indignation in his voice. 'Nothing of the sort, Mr Honeybath. We have kept clear of anything of that kind, I am glad to say. Mr X is no blacker than you are, if it comes to that. Begging your pardon, that is.' Peach had relapsed abruptly into his most distressingly plebeian idiom. 'But I'll tell you something at once. Quite straight, I will. He's out of his mind.'

This time, Honeybath was really astonished.

'Do I understand,' he asked dazedly, 'that you are inviting me to execute the portrait of a lunatic?'

'And why not, Mr Honeybath?' This time, Peach spoke with spirit. 'I don't doubt that others have done it before you. Verynosey, Carpatchy, and all that lot.'

'Possibly so.' Honeybath dimly wondered whether his visitor was a student of *Finnegans Wake*. 'But, if they were, they were undoubtedly constrained to it by tasteless patrons. It is a canon – an absolute canon of art, Mr Peach – that the sheerly pathological is unfit for the purposes of any sort of representative fiction.' Honeybath spoke with dignity. He might have been Sir Joshua Reynolds pronouncing one of his celebrated Discourses. 'The thought, sir, is abhorrent to me.'

'But wouldn't there be a good many mad folk, Mr Honeybath, in Shakespeare and the like? And even in the Bible, if I remember aright.'

'The Bible isn't art. It's history.' Honeybath would not have produced this imperfect reply had he not been a good deal staggered by all this cultural resource on Peach's part. 'And an anonymous zany! It's out of the question. I have my reputation to consider.'

'And very high that is, Mr Honeybath. Otherwise I shouldn't be troubling you. And I assure you that Mr X is a very quiet gentleman – a very quiet and civilly behaved old gentleman indeed. Nothing in the nature of howls and grimaces; nothing of that sort at all. Conversable, in a manner of speaking, Mr X is. Advantages, he's had.' Lesson Six was fading out as Mr Peach strove to carry his point. 'An Eton College boy in his time.'

'Do I understand that he might be described as an Aristocratic Eccentric?' Honeybath was weakening. If these people had money to burn, the sky could be pretty well the limit if one were to undertake so extraordinary a commission. 'And is your Mr X at least sufficiently *compos mentis* himself to desire such a thing?' Honeybath had a brilliant thought. 'Would it be a comfort or consolation to him in his darkened state of mind?'

'Precisely that; sir. Very much that, indeed. It is what is in the relatives' mind. A Christian thought, Mr Honeybath.'

'I see.' Honeybath's hand went out to the sherry decanter. 'You had better tell me a little more about all this.'

'Certainly, Mr Honeybath. Whatever my instructions allow. But confidentiality must be the keynote, if you follow me. And not only in the matter of the gentleman's identity. His place of residence as well.'

2

At this point Charles Honeybath glanced rather desperately round his studio. He might have been Mr Sherlock Holmes (to whom he was addicted) hoping to secure the commonsensical if not wholly percipient counsel of his friend Dr Watson. It was upon just such unlikely missions as Mr Peach's, indeed, that enigmatical plenipotentiaries had been prone to present themselves in Baker Street. Perhaps Mr X wasn't a mere President or Prime Minister. Perhaps he was a Crowned Head, and Honeybath would end up with a pair of diamond cufflinks, the gift of Mr X's second cousin once removed, a Very Gracious Lady. It would be *The Case of the Mysterious Commission.*

Honeybath pulled himself together. He even pushed his own sherry-glass unobtrusively away from him. One obviously needed a clear head. Might not Watson have hinted that they were in the presence of a practical joke? Malicious rivals of Honeybath's – and he laboured, after all, in a crowded vineyard – had got together over their own bottle of wine, and there had been a wager that he could be despatched on a fool's errand. But where on earth had they got hold of a creature like Peach? Perhaps Peach was an out-of-work actor. And here he was, hired to practise upon the innocence of an out-of-work portrait-painter.

These reflections – which at least showed that, at a pinch, Honeybath might prove an adversary of a wariness to be reckoned with – now suggested to him the uses of a protective irony.

'Am I to be conducted into your nameless client's presence,' he asked, 'at the end of a blindfolded journey in a hansom cab?'

'Something of the kind would be a prerequisite, Mr Honeybath.' Peach, recovering his more cultivated manner, enunciated this with the utmost coolness. 'But only after an earnest of the seriousness of our intention. Guineas are a shade awkward when it comes to spot cash. But we can say one thousand pounds down.' With a dexterity suggesting a well-rehearsed effect, Peach produced a bulky wallet from a capacious pocket. He opened it and extracted, one by one, several highly compacted bundles of what were plainly ten-pound notes. These he laid on a table in front of him. 'Shall we count them over?' he asked blandly.

'I think not,' Honeybath said austerely. But he was a good deal shaken. This astonishing display seemed at once to knock the practical-joke or hoax theory out of court. He had only to sweep the notes into a drawer and they did become precisely the earnest Peach had spoken of. He had only to carry them the few yards to his bank next door and they would be recoverable by Peach only at his own, Honeybath's, pleasure. If the banknotes were forgeries (and anything seemed possible in this untoward situation), the teller would probably be sufficiently surprised at receiving so large a sum in this form to scrutinize them with sufficient care to discover the fact. He wouldn't, on the other hand, be astounded, or even venture to ask an old-established customer questions. Honeybath knew that a good many commercial transactions were conducted on just such a cash basis, and that it was not a bank's business to take any initiative in exploring whether some tax-dodging manoeuvre was involved. So now he temporized.

'Do I understand,' he asked, 'that this portrait would not be painted here in my studio?'

'It would not. I hope I have made it clear that a high degree of privacy is required.'

'But there's nobody here except myself. I live elsewhere, and at present I am not employing an assistant of any sort. Your client, if any slight strangeness in him makes it undesirable to attract curiosity, could come and go without the least danger of anything of the kind.'

'It must be a condition, I fear, that the sittings take place in his private residence.'

'And that I don't even know where that is?' Not unnaturally, Honeybath found it hard to accept that anything so melodramatic and absurd as this proviso was being advanced with a seriousness.

'Just that.'

'Very well. I will undertake the commission, Mr Peach. But, until I have familiarized myself with the circumstances, and can be assured that there is nothing scandalously irregular about so strange an arrangement, I shall require to be accompanied by a friend.'

'No.'

'No? Mr Peach, did I hear you aright?'

'Certainly you did. We are trusting you' – Peach pointed uncompromisingly at the banknotes – 'and it's fair that you should trust us.'

Honeybath was baffled. Peach undeniably had a point. Moreover Honeybath doubted whether he himself had a friend in the world to whom he would care to confide the undignified and indeed demeaning bargain he seemed about to accept. But probably – he told himself – he was exaggerating that side of the thing. Sensitive natures such as his were inclined to be touchy. Peach had stated frankly that the prospective sitter was off his head. Perhaps those around him were a bit off their heads too, and it was a dotty sensitiveness of their own which had resulted in the thinking up of all this nonsense. At least he could go and see. And even before he did that, he could perhaps extract at least a modicum of further information from his visitor.

'Provisionally, then,' he said matter-of-factly, 'the affair is settled. We can relax a little, my dear Mr Peach. May I offer you another glass of sherry?'

Peach made no bones about embracing this further modest entertainment. He even raised his glass towards Honeybath and said

'Cheers' before drinking from it. Honeybath, although he might have resented so unwarranted a familiarity, decided to accept the ritual as signalling the establishment of a full measure of confidence between the contracting parties. It seemed the right moment to gather in and lock up the banknotes; and this he now briskly achieved. Peach watched him unconcernedly, even with a distinguishable air of benevolence.

'Would you care to have a receipt, Mr Peach?'

'Dear me, no. Nothing of the kind is at all necessary, sir. But there are one or two questions, if they may be allowed me. Sittings, for example. Would you say that fourteen are likely to be enough?'

'I very much doubt it. My usual procedure – '

'A pity, Mr Honeybath. Really a great pity. It is, you see, for no more than a fortnight that Mr X can be – well, put at your disposal. So it looks as if it won't do, after all.'

'My dear Mr Peach, do you really suppose that I can paint this thing in fourteen days – and work on it every day of the week? You must – '

'Well, yes, Mr Honeybath. I do. It has to be regarded as part of the bargain, I'm afraid.'

'I see.' Honeybath stared at his visitor in what was – far more than at any previous stage of the interview – a sadly divided mind. Could he conceivably regard himself as retaining any shred of professional integrity if he were to allow this staring nonsense to go a single step further? But, of course, there was another way of looking at it. Peach and his principals (whoever they might be) were plainly persons so vastly ignorant of all aesthetic decorum that it was surely admissible to allow oneself a little licence in dealing with them. Between a finished portrait and what might be virtually a sketch in oils they would not have the slightest ability to discriminate. And he could easily lend to his likeness of Mr X the appearance of being little more than a brilliant improvisation. There would be nothing that wasn't entirely respectable about such a frankly bravura affair – particularly as nobody was ever likely to know that he had pocketed two thousand guineas for the thing. And, as there didn't seem to be much prospect of rational pleasure in painting a lunatic (even a harmless lunatic), the sooner the macabre but profitable episode was over the better it would be.

'Very well,' Honeybath said resignedly. 'I'll see what can be done.'

'I'm sure I'm very grateful, sir. As Mr X's relatives will be.'

'Ah, yes – the relatives. Perhaps, Mr Peach, you wouldn't mind telling me – '

'But now another question, Mr Honeybath. If you are likely to feel a little pressed for time, sir, I wonder whether we could assist you in any way? Photographs of Mr X, for example – would they be likely to be of any use to you?'

'Definitely not. I have nothing against the practice of employing photographs, and am aware that many of my most highly reputed colleagues do so.' Honeybath was going into an impressive routine. 'It would be entirely naïve to suppose that a portrait-painter is cheating when he employs such a resource. But it is simply not my habit. I begin by making my own sketches in pencil or crayon. There may be a dozen of them before I think of doing more than merely squaring up the canvas.'

'That's very interesting – very interesting, indeed.' And Peach really did seem genuinely impressed. He was looking sharply at Honeybath. 'On paper, sir, or something of the kind, these sketches would be?'

'Certainly.'

'And they could be passed round? Mr X himself could have the handling of them?'

'There's no reason at all why he should not. Hold on to them, if he cared to.'

'Well, Mr Honeybath, I'll remember that. Something of a child, Mr X is, as I think I've hinted to you. Likes to have something to play with. And to show around.'

'I see.' Honeybath was faintly puzzled by this further twaddle. 'And now, I'm afraid there is at least one question I must ask *you*. Where is this portrait you are requesting me to paint going to hang?'

'To hang?' For the first time, Peach appeared to be taken by surprise, and to find himself stumped for an answer. His instructions, perhaps, hadn't run to this point. 'Is the question material, Mr Honeybath?'

'Of course it's material. The scale of the thing; the pose, whether formal or relaxed; the lighting; the whole compositional key: these are all involved with the matter. You speak of Mr X's relations as arranging the commission, which makes me incline to the supposition that the portrait is destined for a domestic setting. But I may be wrong. For all I know' – Honeybath permitted himself a slight note of asperity – 'your Mr X may be a retired bishop in some more than usually embarrassing stage of mental decay, and the picture destined for Lambeth Palace. Or he may have been a professor of Lord knows what, so that my work will end up in the great hall of Balliol College or Christ Church or in the London Senate House. Or he may have been an Alderman or a Lord Mayor – '

'He certainly hasn't been that, Mr Honeybath.' Peach checked himself, and looked guilty. He had presumably been forbidden to make any positive statement whatever about the shadowy Mr X. 'But I can tell you this. Mr X is to hang in very distinguished company – very distinguished company, indeed. Make no mistake about it. He's been a man right at the top of his class in his time.'

'I'm delighted to hear it.' And it was certainly true that Honeybath's curiosity was pricked. There had, for once, been an unmistakable ring of truth in Peach's voice. He meant what he said. But Honeybath was not, in fact, all that pleased. Two thousand guineas tumbling in during a hard-up spell was quite something, but he still had his reputation to consider. Despite the hugger-mugger nature of the proposed transaction, it was not inconceivable that the portrait was really booked for some august place. He didn't fancy the notion of a skimped and slapdash Honeybath finding itself on a line between a Reynolds and a Gainsborough, or for that matter between a Sutherland and Kokoschka. The mere thought of such a thing turned him cold. He almost saw those banknotes, tucked away so snugly in their drawer, turning to dust and ashes as they lay. 'It must be thought about,' he said rather feebly. 'There must he an interval for reflection, for serious consideration of the decency of the whole thing. I insist on that.'

'Oh, certainly.' Peach was instantly amenable. 'We have till nightfall, after all.'

'I beg your pardon?' Not for the first time in the past half-hour, Honeybath could scarcely believe his ears. 'Did you say *nightfall*?'

'Just that, sir. Mr X's relations are very sensitive about the whole matter. Insanity is always a humiliating thing in a family, wouldn't you say? It oughtn't to be so, but it is so. They insist that Mr X's residence should be approached in the dark. You will agree that it is thoroughly natural, I'm sure.'

There was a short silence – occasioned, it need hardly be said, by Honeybath's inability to find speech. He was obliged hastily to retrieve his sherry and gulp it before contriving further utterance.

'I'm to be taken to this confounded residence, as you call it, in the dark every night, and positively to work under nocturnal conditions?'

'Oh, no – nothing of the kind. We quite understand that you will want to paint in daylight. That's *de rigueur*, I've no doubt.' Peach paused on this expression; he was obviously rather proud of it. 'But you will go, and come away again, in the dark. I can assure you that you will be most comfortably accommodated during your little fortnight. And there's quite a good cook.'

Rather like a man registering stress in a stage comedy, Honeybath had produced a handkerchief and mopped his brow. But although his thoughts may have been confused he really knew that there was only one thing to do. He must fish out those banknotes, chuck them at Peach's irritatingly faceless physiognomy, and order him out of the studio and back to the company of that impressive and patiently waiting chauffeur. And here would be the end of the affair – except, perhaps, that Honeybath would then send for the police. For it could no longer be doubted that there was something uncommonly fishy about the mysterious commission. That was the one true word about it. It had a very fish-like smell.

'So shall we say nine o'clock?' Peach had got to his feet. He had contrived – incredibly he had contrived – to shake hands in a familiar manner with Charles Honeybath. Within seconds, the painter was alone in his studio.

Every man has his price, so Honeybath must have had his. It would be untrue, however, to assert that it had been named that afternoon. Locked in a drawer in his desk, indeed, was a carrot (or the half of a carrot) which had been potent enough through the greater part of his interview with Mr Peach. But that it was continuing to exercise its potency, or to control the situation to the exclusion of other factors, is inconceivable. Charles Honeybath was an educated man; he was, it may be repeated, conscious that he had a reputation to guard; his financial embarrassments were not of the sort that constitute a threat to tomorrow's dinner – or indeed to any subsequent dinner, indefinitely on to the grave. It would be a perfectly well-nourished Honeybath who would eventually present himself for that final banquet at which (as the eminent preacher John Donne once remarked) one is not the feaster but the feasted upon. He was in no state of desperation whatever.

This being so, some other impulse must have been operative in prompting Honeybath to his immediate course of conduct. Perhaps it was intellectual curiosity. He had learned all that was to be learned about portrait-painting – or at least all that was to be learned about it by one who was neither a Rembrandt nor a Velázquez. His range of other interests was not extensive. He was not the type of the socially accomplished artist: a William Rothenstein, say, who has known everybody and has a story about each of them. A childless widower without the inclination to marry again, he was untouched by those domestic exigencies and anxieties which serve to sop up the surplus nervous energies of many men. Again, he had never had a war to speak of; never fought in the warm rain or at the hot gates, bitten by flies. So perhaps – if very obscurely – he was looking for something. Perhaps he was so looking before it was altogether too late; looking for something to satisfy that much younger man who lurks still within many sedate outward presences, who sometimes shouts, soundlessly but urgently, beneath the plummy utterances of established middle age. Or, perhaps again, Honeybath simply obeyed a prompting to make himself a little more interesting to the world than he had been of late. Whatever the truth about Mr X might turn out to be, he promised to provide a story on the strength of which Honeybath could dine out for months ahead.

Any or all of these things may have been true. Certain it is that, later that afternoon, the painter returned to his modest flat, packed a suitcase, left a note for the woman who came in to do for him, dined early in his favourite Italian restaurant, went back to the studio and did some more extensive getting together of the necessities of his craft there.

And it was thus that nine o'clock came round.

3

Punctually the bell rang, and Honeybath went to the door. He expected to be confronted once more by the confidential Peach, but the man before him was the chauffeur. The car, since it was parked under a streetlamp, could be clearly seen, and it was evident that it was empty. There was nothing particularly disconcerting about this, but Honeybath nevertheless found that he was annoyed. He had, after a fashion, got to know Peach, and it had been obscurely in his head that during this drive – whether it was to prove long or short – he could, so to speak, go on with the fellow from where he had left off, and possibly extract at least a few additional scraps of useful information. But perhaps this unexpected state of affairs would actually prove advantageous. He might be able to pump the chauffeur.

'Ah, good evening,' he said, in a cordial but officer-to-man voice. 'Have we much of a drive in front of us?'

'Nothing very out of the way, sir. Would that be your gear?' The chauffeur indicated Honeybath's suitcase and artist's paraphernalia on the floor of the studio. 'They'll go very well in the boot, sir, and be quite safe there.'

'Excellent. Do please bring them out. And the door simply closes behind you.' Honeybath had been visited by a brilliant idea, and one making evident how promisingly there lurked in him the spirit of private detection. He would nip out before this fellow, appear to take an aimless half a dozen paces up and down the pavement, and thereby contrive to acquaint himself with the registration number of the waiting car.

'Thank you, sir. But I'll make you comfortable first.' The chauffeur stood aside for Honeybath and then – as it were shoulder to shoulder – conducted him to a rear door of the vehicle. 'If you will be so good, sir,' he said as he opened it. He might have been a barber of the superior sort, inviting a customer to his seat.

With automatic docility, Honeybath climbed in. The evening was mild, but he hadn't sat down before the chauffeur was enveloping him in a large and opulent fur rug. Then he shut the door and turned back for the luggage. Honeybath, with a feeling which was for the moment almost one of good-natured amusement, realized that he had lost that trick. The chauffeur commanded confidence – at least to the extent that, unlike Mr Peach, he appeared to be exactly what he was. But it was clear enough that he, too, had his instructions. And he had been much too smart for that one about the registration number.

The car, although not of the kind paraded in the interest of prestige and conspicuous expenditure, was large and of the formally conceived sort. The passengers, that is to say, sat in a big glass box and the driver in a little glass box, and communication between the two was by means of some acoustic device which a more rational disposition of things would have rendered unnecessary. Honeybath realized that the prospects of informative chat were not too good.

He could, on the other hand, at least look around undisturbed. The chauffeur could scarcely suggest blindfolding him, or throw a blanket over his head in the manner favoured by the police when conducting hither or thither some unfortunate individual who has been helping them with their inquiries. Nor did the car have blinds all round, since that was an amenity which had gone out more or less with dear old Queen Mary. Honeybath, who knew his London very well, had little doubt that he could retain a pretty sound knowledge of where this wild-goose affair was taking him. He settled himself comfortably in his seat. The chauffeur was stowing his stuff in the back. It was observable that he took even more care of Honeybath's professional equipment than of his merely diurnal baggage. This showed tact. It even showed something like refined feeling. A slight sense of personal importance stole over Honeybath. He was glad that it had occurred to him to pack his dinner-jacket. Odd as this affair was, it might nevertheless be bringing him into the company of people with civilized habits.

The chauffeur took his seat, and the car moved off. Nothing could be easier, Honeybath told himself, than to keep an eye on the route. At the moment it looked very much as if the fellow was making for Millbank. This was something which Honeybath himself, when setting out from his studio, would do only if he was proposing to cross Lambeth Bridge. There was the possibility, however, that the car was going to proceed very deviously to its destination, and eventually plunge into some obscure quarter which there was almost no chance of his knowing about. But this, on the whole, seemed unlikely; they could scarcely be proposing to put him up for a fortnight (and even supply the services of quite a good cook) in a South or East London slum. And if he did lose his bearings for a time, couldn't he simply command the chauffeur to stop at a tobacconist's, or something of that kind? He could then manage a swift reconnaissance, or at least ask the man in the shop for his bearings. The chauffeur, presumably, would hardly risk disobeying so small an injunction; to do so would be to be putting his passenger too nakedly under duress.

But how, in the first instance, did one communicate with the chauffeur? The answer seemed to lie in a microphone-like contraption which depended from a bracket on Honeybath's right hand. He picked it up, and at once a small informative light went on at the top of it.

'Can you hear me?' he asked of this thing.

'Yes, sir – for so long as you hold the instrument. Can I be of any assistance to you?'

'No, no – nothing of the kind. It has just occurred to me to ask you whether you happen to know if Chelsea won their match.'

'Yes, sir. Two-Nil.'

'Thank you very much.' Honeybath replaced the microphone, and reflected with satisfaction that he had extracted at least some information from the fellow. Not precisely relevant information. But it was a start. He sank back again on his seat, and as he did so he pushed away the fur rug. It was a good deal too hot in the car, and he must by no means turn drowsy. He decided to lower a window and let in some fresh air. But the windows appeared to be unprovided with the ordinary sort of crank for this purpose. Probably the job was done by some totally unnecessary electrical push-button affair. It was with the irritation of the artist in the face of pretentious and trivial technology that Honeybath again picked up the microphone. 'These windows,' he demanded, ' – how do they open and shut?'

'Full air-conditioning in the interior, sir. Do you require a little more warmth?'

'Nothing of the kind. It's much too hot as it is.'

'The small red illuminated arrow in front of you, sir. Turn it to point at the small blue light, and you will get cooler air at once.'

'Thank you.' Honeybath once more replaced the microphone, and then located the red illuminated arrow. He rotated the switch within which it glowed until it duly pointed at the small blue light. It was an idiotic performance, he reflected, and one could only be alarmed that the sort of people who bought this kind of car must be of a mental age of round about twelve. Fantasies of space travel were what such gimmicks catered for.

But at least the affair was efficient. Cool air blew in at once – so that Honeybath fleetingly registered the thought that he was going to be much more alert to his situation than he had been moments before. But the cool air had two odd properties. It had a faint smell. And it seemed to turn cold, not cool, as it touched his face.

And this was Charles Honeybath's last discovery about the limousine (as it was probably called) transporting him to the residence (as it had been styled) of Mr X. He was comfortably unconscious for the rest of the journey.

'Enjoyed your nap, sir?' the chauffeur asked solicitously. He was assisting Honeybath up a flight of steps. The last thing of which Honeybath had been aware was a smell – and very far down in him now was an unslumbering intelligence which again made an appeal to his nose. Here, briefly, was open air again. Town air, or country air? The question itself was an achievement. Unfortunately Honeybath's nose returned no answer at all. He was feeling relaxed, confused, and ever so slightly sick. 'This door, sir,' he heard the chauffeur say.

'Odd little room.' Honeybath made this comment without displeasure, and as the most simple observation upon his immediate surroundings.

'Not a room, sir. An elevator.' The chauffeur spoke kindly, without the faintest hint of mockery. 'I believe you'll find your quarters very comfortable. And I'll see to it they have up your gear in no time.' And the chauffeur, whose peaked cap was respectfully in his hand, touched a button – one more button – and sliding doors smoothly closed on Charles Honeybath. It was the kind of lift which harbours no chink to peer through, and the acceleration and de-acceleration of which is so exquisitely controlled that gravity, baffled, delivers no message at all. Honeybath might have been ascending to the top of a skyscraper. Or he might simply have been going up one storey.

Thus for some moments in solitude and unobserved, he had one of his brilliant ideas. He didn't know where he'd been brought, but he could at least work out how long the drive had taken. He glanced swiftly at his watch. Its hands pointed to seven o'clock. He knew perfectly well that he couldn't have been asleep or unconscious for nearly ten hours. The watch had been monkeyed with – and presumably while still on his wrist. He felt a novel sensation which he was constrained to identify as fear. His life had been sheltered; it is probable that he hadn't been thus visited since his first week at private school. The feeling passed.

The doors of the lift opened upon what polite writers used to call an impassive manservant. He might have been the chauffeur's elder brother. His clothes were inky (but the word invites misunderstanding; rather, they were inken), and he conveyed the semi-obliterated effect, the air of preserving inviolable at some remote depth everything not required of him as a consequence of his menial employment, which is the special quality of superior domestics.

'May I show you to your room, sir?' The man accompanied this question with a bow so restrained that it might have been offered by one diplomat to another on the most frigid of international occasions. It seemed to Honeybath that one thing was clear: whatever he was involved in was genuinely a high-life affair. The theory of the practical joke or wager briefly recurred to him. He had become the pawn of people so incredibly self-confident and arrogant and wealthy that they thought nothing of chucking away a very large sum of money in the interest of a tiresome and perhaps humiliating jape. And 'jape' was precisely the word: it had the right Edwardian ring.

This thought, although not agreeable, at least offered a measure of reassurance. By plunging in rather than backing out he had at least not put himself to any major hazard – as he might have done, for example, had he with a similar regardlessness placed himself within the power of a solitary madman. Apart from Mr X himself, there could be no question of serious madness, whether harmless or otherwise, significantly involved. Even if Peach and the chauffeur and this suave major-domo were all crooks (which was a most extravagant supposition), they could scarcely have bound themselves to the service of a wealthy maniac. The practical joke might, of course, later reveal itself as having some thoroughly nasty edge; in (again) the Edwardian era, as during the Regency, such things used sometimes to take a sadistic rather than a merely malicious turn. But this was surely an unnecessarily alarmist view. He might be put in a reputedly haunted room and harried by bogus ghosts: something of that kind. He was unlikely to be beaten senseless, or hunted by savage dogs, or chucked into a bottomless well.

Whether these were comforting reflections or not, they didn't remain with Honeybath for long. The manservant had opened a door, and was standing aside for him to enter. Here was his room.

He didn't much take to it. It was large, and in several ways hinted itself to his experienced eye as belonging to a substantial mansion of the Georgian period. The *décor* was expensive, and the furniture – bedroom-like at one end and with a lavish effect of sitting-around ease at the other – was expensive too. It would have been unjust to say that, either as a whole or in its parts, anything but good taste was evident. But it was impersonal good taste – which is almost a contradiction in terms. It had all been put together by somebody who made his living that way. And Honeybath had seen it – had seen the identical kind of thing, that is – before. It was what you found in a country house which has been taken over by some great industrial corporation and refurbished regardless of cost for the lavish entertainment of top-ranking foreign customers. If it was really something of this kind that he had stumbled upon – he reflected without much satisfaction – then Peach's 'quite a good cook' was likely to prove a considerable understatement.

'May I ask, sir, whether you have already dined?'

'Yes, certainly I have.' Honeybath had emerged from his perplexed cogitations with a start.

'Would you care to have a light supper served here in your room?'

'Thank you, no – nothing of the kind.' Honeybath had now spotted, on a table at the far end of the room, an array of bottles and decanters which were too numerous to look quite in place, but which suggested comfort, all the same.

'Your bathroom, sir.' The man had discreetly opened a farther door. His tone politely deprecated the tenuousness of Honeybath's material needs. 'Mr Arbuthnot has asked me to say that he will look in during the next quarter of an hour.'

'Mr Arbuthnot?' No doubt absurdly, Honeybath was almost startled at hearing a proper name thus enunciated. He would have expected 'Mr Y' or 'Mr Z'.

'Yes, sir. He will wish to assure himself that you have had a comfortable journey. And I will myself wish you good night.'

The manservant withdrew, closing the door with professional noiselessness behind him. Honeybath wondered whether he had locked it as well. But he didn't, for the moment, try to find out. Instead, he walked over to the drinks and grabbed the brandy. It was certainly an occasion for that.

4

The brandy was not of the sort into which ice should be chucked and soda water splashed, but Honeybath nevertheless performed these actions. It comforted him to behave as one might behave in a hotel at the end of a tiresome day. He even frowned in displeasure that the brandy and everything else was not – as one expects it to be in a high-category hotel nowadays – neatly stored in one's private refrigerator.

He turned, glass in hand, to take a better look at his room, and his first discovery was a Monet hanging opposite the bed. He was in a good deal startled. Claude Monet lived for eighty-six years, and during seventy of them he painted like mad. The world's Monets are therefore very numerous indeed. But even more numerous are those individuals and institutions eager to have top Impressionists on their walls (or in their yachts). Monets are thus extremely costly. Honeybath was confirmed in the persuasion that he had mysteriously become the prisoner of some vast corporation: Shell, perhaps, or ICI, or General Motors – something like that. The Monet represented nebulous water-lilies in an indeterminate pool. Honeybath contemplated it in some gloom. Here he was, fixated for good in mid-career with disgusting fleshy objects – of which Mr X would presently prove to be a banal example. Young Monet had broken away from all that – or, rather, he had just refused to take up with it. Finally, he had simply cultivated his garden – his own water-garden, in the most literal sense – and there was nothing wrong with his lilies except that they were a good deal larger than life. To refuse to be more than an eye or to paint anything except light: these have been the inspired means of becoming a swell in the 1870s. Some equivalent inspiration was doubtless just round the corner a hundred years later. But it wouldn't be Charles Honeybath who would discover it.

These were reflections irrelevant to his present situation, and it struck him he would be better employed looking not at the Monet but out of the window. Or out of either of the windows, since the room had two of these in one of its longer walls. Curtains falling from ceiling to floor were now drawn across them, and probably concealed embrasures of some depth. He crossed the room to the nearer window and slipped behind the curtain. He could now just distinguish a lowered blind. Groping for its cord, he let the blind up gently. He was gazing into darkness. Unless what was before him was the well of an unlit building, it seemed certain that he was in the depth of the countryside. He looked upward. A few stars were visible, but nothing of the glow which London projects upon the night sky. But nearer what must be the line of the horizon he could distinguish, as his vision accommodated itself to the nocturnal scene, dim masses of deeper darkness which he knew could only be trees. it seemed probable that, from the elevation of at least a second storey, he was looking out over a park. And there wasn't a sound. With traffic as it was nowadays, it seemed improbable that there could be a main road within miles.

Then suddenly there *was* a sound, although it didn't come from a car or lorry. What Honeybath heard was the characteristic racket, not easy to describe, of a fast-moving train: a muted clatter as of innumerable far-away doors rattling in a wind. The sound increased, and now – straight ahead – there appeared a streak of light like a fiery spear skimming the ground. The sound grew louder still and the stream of light grew brighter: against it could be seen in silhouette the trunks of trees hurtling by. A moment more, and the whole phenomenon had faded – but there could be no doubt that a railway-line ran surprisingly close to what Peach had liked to call Mr X's residence.

There was again complete silence outside. Honeybath decided if possible to open the window in front of him – this in order to peer out and determine his height above the ground. But to manage this he had to see what he was about, and it thus became necessary to turn round, draw back the curtain, and admit adequate light to the restricted area within which he stood. The action, when achieved, was of unexpected effect. He found himself face to face with an elderly man in evening-dress, who had apparently been about to perform the same operation on the curtain from its other side. What is called in stage parlance a discovery had thus been achieved simultaneously by both parties.

'My dear Mr Honeybath, how do you do?' The stranger had extended a cordial but not over-eager hand. 'I am Basil Arbuthnot. How good of you to have fallen in with our plans so handsomely. And to have come straight away! You must have had to drop all sorts of important things. It has really been quite beyond our expectation. We are *most* grateful.'

Mr Arbuthnot delivered himself of all this without the least effect of haste or of the garrulous. He had a small pointed beard turning grey; his smoking-jacket was an affair of faded maroon velvet and dim maroon silk; he would have looked very well if posed against a baronial background in the interest of one of the more expensive brands of malt whisky.

'I do hope,' he went on, 'that you had a pleasant run? A pity there is no moon. Perhaps it was the moon that you were glancing out of the window in search of? Or the pole star, or something like that?'

'The pole star would do to be going on with, Mr Arbuthnot.' Honeybath had decided to speak robustly. 'If I'm looking for my bearings, you can't be exactly surprised. You won't be unaware, sir, that you've involved me in an uncommonly odd situation.'

'But indeed yes! I do fully understand your feeling. But we are a whimsical family, I suppose, and you must bear with us.'

'A family? Is this person you are pleased to call Mr X related to you?'

'The poor fellow is my uncle, Mr Honeybath. But shall we sit down?' Arbuthnot had turned back into the room. 'Not that I must play the host in what are to be your own quarters. *You* are the one to do that.'

'Then let me get you a drink,' Honeybath said rather shortly. This punctilio hadn't particularly amused him. And he was beginning to feel distinctly tired.

'Marc, if you please – and no more than a dash of it.' Mr Basil Arbuthnot sank down in a chair in a thoroughly relaxed way. Then he anxiously straightened up again. 'But shall I be boring you, if I start to tell you all about ourselves? Shall we put off anything of the kind until tomorrow?'

'Certainly not. The sooner I hear a little sense about this uncle of yours the better.' Honeybath poured Arbuthnot his drink, uncomfortably conscious of having employed a discourteous form of words. This was highly absurd – for hadn't he, after all, virtually been kidnapped? But the feeling was inescapable. 'About your uncle,' he said, stonily and by way of correction. And he poured himself a little more brandy.

'Then let us have at least a preliminary talk at once.' Arbuthnot smiled with the most perfect candour. 'And would it be most satisfactory if you simply asked me questions?'

'I've no reason to suppose so. It wasn't a method that got much out of that fellow Peach.'

'Peach?' Arbuthnot was momentarily at sea. 'Ah, yes! Peach had his instructions, of course. But you and I can allow ourselves a little more freedom, Honeybath, don't you think?'

'Very well.' Honeybath wasn't at all sure that he had cared for this familiar form of address. 'You say your name's Arbuthnot. Why the dickens should you insist that your uncle be called Mr X?'

'Ah, an excellent question. There's a harmless enough reason, which I'll be delighted to explain to you.'

'And so you want me positively to address him as Mr X?'

'Well, no. It might conceivably puzzle him. Indeed, it might annoy him. In fact, my dear sir, you'd greatly oblige us all by addressing him as *Mon Empereur*.'

'As *what*?'

'*Mon Empereur.* My uncle believes himself, unhappily, to be Napoleon Bonaparte. It's something quite common, we are told, among persons of his – um – way of thinking.'

'Certainly it can't be called very inventive,' Honeybath said dryly. Whether rationally or not, he really was a little disappointed at this information about Mr X. When one is virtually press-ganged into giving a substantial span of time to painting a lunatic, one may surely hope for a subject with a slightly less commonplace delusion than this. 'Will he be dressed in the Corsican ruffian's clothes?'

'Oh, no – nothing like that. It's all, you may say, no more than inside my poor uncle's head. We don't have to stage a court for him, or anything of that sort – as in some play or other I remember seeing once. By Strindberg, would it have been?'

'Pirandello, I imagine.' Honeybath's patience was wearing thin. 'Have you really anything relevant to tell me, Mr Arbuthnot, or are you merely putting in a little time talking round the thing?'

'Honeybath, my dear fellow, just give me a chance.' Arbuthnot said this with an urbanity so unruffled, and so charming a smile, that Honeybath found himself almost taking to the man. 'I have to pick my words, you know – because of certain pledges I have given to some needlessly nervous kinsmen. But I am most anxious to be perfectly open with you. You are entitled to complete frankness, and complete frankness you shall receive.' Arbuthnot made a resigned gesture. 'Aside, that is, from one or two necessary reservations. But here, for a start, is the nub of the whole matter. My uncle is supposed to be dead.'

'Whereas, if there is to be a portrait, I suppose it is a matter of *Vive l'Empereur.*' Honeybath was rather pleased with this witticism – which, indeed, was extremely well received by Mr Arbuthnot.

'Precisely so,' Arbuthnot said. 'You make the point most felicitously. A portrait we all feel we must have, and my uncle must be brought alive for the purpose. But only very cautiously, and on a strictly temporary basis. Not a breath of his brief resurrection must reach the public. Hence the precautions we have felt constrained to take.'

This time, Honeybath remained silent. There was something thoroughly indecent, he told himself, in this riddling and quibbling talk about a mentally afflicted man, and he ought not for a moment to have allowed himself to joke about it. And Arbuthnot must have been aware of this reaction, for he now assumed a serious expression.

'He was a remarkable man, my dear Honeybath. One ought not, of course, to speak of him in the past tense – and yet one does so, almost inevitably. His career now seems to belong to a vanished age. Or, rather, his careers seem to do that. For he was a notably versatile person. He was undoubtedly the best amateur golfer of his day, and equally undoubtedly among its three or four most distinguished mountaineers. And these distinctions formed, surely, a tolerably unusual prelude to a Nobel Prize.'

'What did he get that for?'

'Ah, I must not be too specific. We have given certain pledges – those of us in the family who want this portrait – to those others who are rather misdoubting about it. I mustn't say anything – and I assure you this does embarrass me very much – which might lead to an identification of your sitter.' Arbuthnot produced his easiest smile. It was perfectly evident that embarrassment was among the human frailties unknown to him. 'For example, I must not, I feel, divulge to you whether or not my uncle has received the Order of Merit. If I said he has, it would rather narrow things down, would it not? But his distinction was of that calibre. Naturally, we are very proud of him.'

'Naturally you are – and I suppose your wanting a portrait is a way of showing it. But I'm bound to say I don't understand why, as a family, you should be so keen on having him supposed dead.'

'It does appear to call for a word of explanation, I agree. So what shall I say? At least you may exclude – what I am sure will be a great relief to you – the more psychopathological motivations. The death-wish within the family, and things of that sort. On the contrary, I think I can honestly claim that we are a devoted little clan. Again, it had nothing to do with missing heirs, lost wills, unmentionable vices, or anything of the sort. You may be absolutely reassured, my dear fellow, as to that.'

Honeybath wondered how much of what Arbuthnot said he was at all seriously expected to swallow. The speculation prompted another sip at his brandy, but this afforded him little comfort. The brandy was Arbuthnot's brandy, and drinking it simply enhanced his sense of having got himself into a false position. It would be impossible to maintain that he had been dragged into the depths of the countryside and tumbled into this unaccountable mansion while vigorously screaming, biting and scratching. He had come of his own free will, and upon a very substantial financial consideration. This chatter, so far, was dawning on him as an insulting diet of poppycock. But it wasn't being offered so crudely that he could very reasonably stand up and walk out (or attempt to walk out – since the sense of an element of all but naked imprisonment was growing on him). But at least he could maintain a note not too abjectly accommodating.

'Look here,' he said, 'I really must be treated to *some* sense. I accept it that your uncle's nervous state is such that you want this portrait-painting to be a very quiet affair. I even accept the implication – although it is an outrageous one – that you cannot safely trust my discretion not to go round the clubs and pubs making a funny story out of you – so that I must leave as I have come, not knowing who the devil any of you really are. But this business of your uncle having to be brought back briefly from the dead – ' Honeybath hesitated for a moment; it was not for the first time that words were in danger of failing him. 'It's just a bit too much, you know. You say you're going to explain it. Will you kindly do so?'

'My dear fellow, I'm on the verge of precisely that!' The urbane character calling himself (no doubt wholly faithlessly) Basil Arbuthnot looked innocently surprised. 'It's merely a matter of coming a little along the road of our Mr X's notable career. To all the business in – well, I'll call it Outer Mongolia. Not that it *was* Outer Mongolia. There! You see how absolutely candid I'm being with you.'

'I think I'm coming to estimate your candour accurately enough. But go on. Just for the moment, it's all I ask.'

'I can see that my uncle's very eminence – which I could so easily have concealed from you – must make the fact and character of his mission almost implausible. I grant that most freely. But consider! He was the one man in England with the authority and the knowledge to put it through. And the courage, I can honestly add. The danger, the strain, the long drawn-out concentration required must be evident in the issue – in the issue, that's to say, on its unhappy, and not on its blessedly triumphant, side. It cost him his reason. I don't see that you could ask for fuller proof than that.'

'Do I understand you to be asserting that your uncle, after scaling unknown peaks – '

'In Outer Mongolia – yes.'

' – and collecting a Nobel Prize, and being enrolled, or just not enrolled, by command of the Sovereign, among the twenty-four Members of the Order of Merit, then started in as a secret agent, or something of that kind?'

'Very much something of that kind. He got what was needed. He got it *out*. And then they caught him, and gave him a very bad time. In the end, they simply buried him, without much troubling themselves as to whether he was actually already dead or not. That's their charming way, no doubt. And he *wasn't* dead.'

'He unburied himself?'

'The job was done for him by a pack of jackals, or hyenas, or obliging creatures of that sort. And then he crawled for hundreds of miles. Finally – '

'You can spare me the finality, Mr Arbuthnot.' Honeybath was rather pleased with this. 'It became expedient that dead it should continue to be?'

'Just so. You are admirably quick, my dear Honeybath.'

'And he is admirably dead to this moment?'

'Alas, yes. It had to be so. There were considerations of high policy, of *very* high policy. And remember that his mind was irrevocably darkened. It was obvious that the remainder of his days must be passed in total seclusion. So the course adopted was really the most humane thing. Inevitably, however, his nearest and dearest had to know – and to arrange for caring for him. But it's really no burden. You'll find him a most charming old man.' Arbuthnot paused. He evidently felt that he was concluding on a truly sunny note. 'By the way, would you care for a hot-water bottle? There is, of course, an electric blanket of the thermostatic kind. But some prefer the old-fashioned thing. I confess I do myself.' Arbuthnot rose gracefully to his feet. 'And I've kept you up far too long. Believe me, I do apologize.'

Honeybath hadn't needed a hot-water bottle. He didn't need the thermostatic blanket either. The whole bedroom was a damned sight too thermostatic. It was like an excessively well-appointed madhouse cell. Lying in its darkness, he came to wonder whether, when they buried him, they might not be a shade careless as to his being already dead too. More temperately, he realized that, at the end of an excessively trying day, he had been subjected for half an hour to the play of an alarmingly insolent and morbid sense of humour. He tried to persuade himself that he at least retained a certain intellectual curiosity as to what sort of person Mr X would really turn out to be. But he had to acknowledge that, through what would certainly prove to be a sleepless night, there wasn't going to be much room in his consciousness for anything except humiliating apprehensiveness over his mere personal safety. He'd been chucked into something like an idiotic tale of terror by Edgar Allan Poe.

Somewhere out in the night, a clock struck eleven. It might be a church clock, a stable clock: impossible to tell. There was a hitch, a muted effect – he mechanically noted – on the ninth stroke. A little later, and again with that effect of being surprisingly near at hand, a railway engine produced a rising and then swiftly declining wail. It was a Diesel engine – the sound from which is even eerier and more discomfiting in the night than used to be that from the steam engines of an earlier day. Then midnight struck, and with the same odd acoustic effect as before.

Very unexpectedly, Charles Honeybath went to sleep after all.

5

Artists tell us – or at least some artists do – that painting absolutely anything is like performing the act of love. One's subject may be a heap of turnips or a pair of old boots, but with these one is interfusing one's own deepest being as one works. This is perhaps a highly coloured view of the matter, and one which chiefly reflects the curiously pan-sexual slant of our modern thinking. But be this as it may, it is certainly possible for a painter, *qua* painter, to fall in love at first sight. That Honeybath did so – of course in a loose and figurative sense – with the strange old creature Mr X proved to be must be held to account for the fact that, after all, he settled in with tolerable satisfaction to the assignment which had so bizarrely and uncomfortably come to him.

But even before he glimpsed Mr X, his sense of personal peril had abated. It scarcely survived, indeed, the manservant – a younger and less impressive, but still admirably trained manservant – who had entered his room on the first morning, drawn back the curtains, raised the blinds, deferentially enunciated the time of day and the state of the weather, deposited morning tea and a copy of *The Times* at his bedside, inquired whether he should draw a bath, and withdrawn upon the information that breakfast too was served to Mr Arbuthnot's guests in their rooms. Honeybath was a man sensitive to these minor graces of life commanded by the well-to-do. So now, when the China tea turned out to be of a quality to the achieving of which Mr Fortnum and Mr Mason in committee might be conceived as having given anxious thought, his confidence in the universe (and in that central feature of it known as Charles Honeybath) was in substantial measure restored to him.

This didn't prevent him, as soon as the young man had departed, from jumping out of bed and making his way to a window. He was like a mariner who, while finding his desert island unexpectedly prolific in amenity, yet feels that there would be reassurance in even a distant sail. But there wasn't a sail; there was just a park.

A park – a gentleman's or nobleman's park – is a comfortable thing. Find such a prospect outside one's weekend window, and one's innocent imagination at once identifies oneself with the ownership of it. Here, at last, are one's own broad acres!

Not all parks, of course, constitute broad acres in themselves, although they may suggest an agricultural hinterland which may be so described. Honeybath, in his time, had looked out on parks which were in themselves very extensive indeed – for he had painted a duke or two now and then, and it is not to be expected of such grandees that they should clock in at a Chelsea studio. It was on the basis of this experience that he was able to tell himself at once that this park was a modest sort of park. Here was the kind of effect which, in the eighteenth century, country gentlemen whose taste (and pretensions) exceeded their rent-rolls contrived out of a stream, a duck-pond, and a coppice or two within which a few oaks and beeches usefully spread a lordly shade. It was all very pleasant, even august in a moderate way, but it didn't exactly extend, vista by vista, far beyond a middle distance. At the moment, indeed, the vista was closed (as the landscape gardeners used to say) by a railway-train. And the railway-train, like the rest of the prospect, was in a static state.

It was also the only visible object to have been created other than directly by the deity. And here is a fact about parks. They needn't be all that extensive in order to occlude the view of anything other than themselves. You may be able to spot a church tower appearing above one or another grassy swell amid the groves. But then again you may not. On this occasion, it was not. There were just trees, and some sheep, and this railway-train. And now the railway-train went away. It appeared to have been arrested at some rural halt well below its accustomed station in life; to have resented the fact; and now, upon its release by some invisible signal, to be eager to resume its own bright speed once more. As it accelerated, Honeybath was just able to remark, here and there upon its flashing sides, certain small yellow rectangles which he knew must carry the name of its destination. But even if the train had still been immobile it would have been quite impossible to decipher this with the naked eye. Nor, when the train had departed, was anything informative revealed. Behind the railway-line there were simply more trees. What the poet calls blessed seclusion from this jarring world appeared to be the eminent characteristic of Honeybath's temporary and enforced residence.

The improvised studio provided for him was also secluded. It lay at a short remove from his own room, at the end of a corridor which appeared otherwise wholly unfrequented. Mr X came up in the lift. Or rather he was brought up in the lift, since his great age now confined him to an invalid chair. He had a female attendant who was introduced to Honeybath as Sister Agnes – which was a style which seemed somehow to suggest less a trained nurse than a devout person who has entered religion. Sister Agnes may have been devout. She was certainly grim, and had to be presumed devoted – this if only because she never let her patient out of her sight.

Honeybath wondered whether Mr X might be suicidally inclined. He also wondered – and with rather more professional interest – whether he *was* of great age. Was he in his middle nineties, or only in his middle sixties? It seemed incredible that an expert in at least the tangible and visible surfaces of human life should be at sea about this. Honeybath had sometimes reflected that, if the worst came to the worst and commissions simply dried up altogether, he could make a very decent living as that sort of fairground character who guesses your age and returns your money plus a whiff of candy-floss if he gets it more than two years wrong. With Mr X he might be astray by more than twenty.

This was beguiling in itself. It also almost persuaded him that, unlikely as it seemed, Arbuthnot's biographical sketch of his relative had not been wholly a pack of lies. Dire experience of no common sort might produce just such an enigma. Mr X could have spent twenty years in a dungeon, dieted exclusively on potatoes, bread and lard – or an equal number of hours impaled on an anthill, or being otherwise disagreeably treated to a limit of human endurance. His pallor was extraordinary, was in itself a daunting challenge to the palette. He had brilliant dark-ringed eyes, a short sharp nose, a mean mouth, and a single lock of lank hair, still with trace of colour to it, depending over a domed forehead. Perhaps because he was of necessity precluded from all physical exercise, he was also a paunchy little man. And he sat with two fingers of his right hand thrust between the buttons of a crumpled waistcoat. There wasn't the slightest difficulty in addressing him as *Mon Empereur*. It seemed the most natural thing in the world.

Not that it was more than infrequently that Mr X demanded this. His sense of his exalted identity – or, for that matter, of any identity at all – was intermittent. Conceivably he was, although again intermittently, aware of this ultimate mystery about himself, and put in substantial spells brooding over it. At these times there was a questing look in his eyes, a yearning to plumb some abysm, to bridge some chasm, which it had come to Honeybath to know, almost at the first glance, as representing his own chance of glory. Get *this* on canvas successfully, and it would be with awe that future generations would murmur his name. Leonardo's sphinx-like lady in the Louvre simply wouldn't be in the competition.

It was in this fond persuasion that Honeybath set to work.

'Able was I ere I saw Elba,' Mr X murmured. The thought appeared just to have struck him. 'Or St Helena, for that matter, my dear Monsieur David.' (Mr X frequently addressed Honeybath by this interesting name.) 'It was a most damnable mistake ever to mount the deck of that confounded *Bellerophon*. The English sailors, by the way, called it the *Billy Ruffian*. Rather amusing that, eh?' Mr X sometimes had a most charming smile.

'I hope they made you comfortable?' Quite early in the series of sittings, Honeybath had found himself chatting with Mr X easily enough. Once one has taken the plunge of humouring insanity it proves a surprisingly simple matter.

'It was better than the *Northumberland*, which I made the final voyage on.' Mr X was well clued up on his own phantasmal history; there was solid reading behind it. 'But I didn't at all take to that Captain Maitland. I addressed him as Captain Ruffian, as a matter of fact. He didn't like it at all. A most undistinguished officer, I imagine, but prided himself on being quite the polished diplomat. Wilks, now, was all right. He knew that the beastly little island was at least *my* island. But they packed him off in no time, and introduced that intolerable Hudson Lowe.'

Honeybath was about to say: 'Who kept the job, didn't he, till your death?' But he refrained. When Mr X became agitated and incoherent Sister Agnes was apt to produce a hypodermic. Honeybath disliked that. Besides which, experiments on the mad are best left to the mad-doctors. They are barred to an amateur – or at least to an amateur with the instincts of a gentleman. Honeybath soothingly requested a slight turning of the head. A few minutes later he handed Mr X a pencil sketch. 'I expect,' he said, 'you may like to see how we are getting on.'

'Not up to your Distribution of the Eagles, Monsieur David.' Mr X said this with imperial frankness. 'Or to my favourite – the one in which I am pointing the way to Italy. However, it's very well in its way. I am pleased to retain it for the archive.' Mr X stuffed the drawing deftly beneath his behind. 'With your permission, Monsieur,' he added graciously.

Honeybath silently bowed his gratification. He was quite getting into the spirit of the thing. And it was rather amusing to be taken for Jacques Louis David.

He even came to accept with a good grace the curious routine of his day. All his meals were served to him in the solitude of his room, but Arbuthnot appeared from time to time and made conversation. Occasionally they went down in the lift together and into the open air. He saw little of the house on the way, and nothing of its other inhabitants. Perhaps, apart from the eminently respectable domestics, there weren't any. Or perhaps all Mr X's anxious and affectionate relations lived here, but were taking care to keep out of his way. It was written into the record, after all, that they were a pathologically secretive crowd. As for the breather *en plein air*, that took place in a walled garden, and so wasn't informative. At times all this built up into a decidedly claustrophobic effect. If Honeybath hadn't been absorbed in his portrait – so absorbed as really to be in an exceptional mental state – he wouldn't have stood it as easily as he did.

As it was, he became secretive in his own way. At times he had a strong impulse to furtive exploration. But the only territory he could explore was his own room. He poked about in drawers and climbed up to peer at the tops of cupboards. But all this yielded very little. If the room was normally in any sort of use, every sign of the fact had been effectively rubbed out before he was dumped in it.

At length, however, he did come on something. Between the two windows, and against the wall, was a Hepplewhite tambour writing-table, with its drawers, big and little, as empty as if it were in a shop. But depressions in the carpet suggested that it had formerly stood a few feet farther out in the room, and Honeybath had the curiosity to restore it to this position. The result was to expose to view a single shallow drawer at the back. He opened this, and what he found was mildly perplexing. The drawer contained a couple of vulgarly erotic magazines, a map of Central London upon which somebody had here and there drawn small circles in red ink, a forbidding-looking textbook on what appeared to be obscure metallurgical processes, and a pair of remarkably high-grade binoculars.

Honeybath had no impulse to edify himself with the reading-matter, whether heavy or light. He saw no interest in the map. But the binoculars were a tremendous find. This was because of the trains. If he wanted to know where he was – even remotely where he was – the trains passing to and fro just beyond the park seemed to be his only hope. The majority of them went flashing by, and about these nothing could be done. But just occasionally, as he had earlier remarked with interest, a train did stop, although very briefly, in full view. These binoculars could have the effect of bringing such a train within a few yards of him. He had only to be patient, and one of those informative yellow rectangles would yield its secret. He would know on just what main line – for a main line it certainly was – this nameless mansion lay.

It is possible that Honeybath was a little taken aback by the excitement which his small discovery occasioned in him; by the thoroughly juvenile sense, as it seemed, of having gained a trick, possessed himself of a secret weapon. He found himself reflecting that he must be careful not to use the binoculars at a time when the young manservant might come into the room and discover him to be so employed. This was absurd – just as absurd as that he didn't at times say things like 'This afternoon I intend to go out and explore the countryside a little'. Why didn't he, at least, test out his position by such means? The answer was, of course, that he was frightened. In part, he was frightened of something ruthless which he felt lurking pervasively in his mysterious environment. But he was now even more frightened, oddly enough, merely of upsetting things. Because what was going forward on the canvas in his painting-room was more important than anything else whatever.

He discovered that the possibility of being detected while peering through the binoculars simply didn't arise. Strangely perhaps, he had failed to reflect that his bathroom window must command exactly the same view as his bedroom windows. The bathroom window was, quite absurdly, a frosted affair – as if modesty required that the naked human form should be screened from the regard even of the stars or the angels. This was perhaps why the simple fact of the matter hadn't struck him at once. He had only to lock himself in, throw up the sash, and do as much spying as he pleased.

He didn't, so far as his immediate object went, have to do a great deal. Actually the first train to appear was so obliging as to draw to a halt with a couple of its carriages neatly centred in that convenient gap at the border of the park. On one of these carriages hung the yellow rectangle. And on the yellow rectangle, and to be read with no difficulty at all, was the single word *Swansea*.

So that was it. Mr X's residence – if it was indeed in any honest sense his – lay only a few hundred yards from the main line of what used to be called the Great Western Railway.

Rightly or wrongly, this appeared to Honeybath to be a momentous discovery, the mere making of which reflected credit on his own enterprise and perspicacity. How many men would have thought to move a writing-table out from the wall, on the chance of discovering a neglected drawer and something significant hidden in it? It was positively what you might expect a professional detective to do!

He worked particularly effectively at the sitting that afternoon. He made a small but significant discovery in the mastoid-temporal area of Mr X's skull. He saw that the two fingers thrust into Mr X's waistcoat (leaving six plus thumbs to be depicted gratis) were going to prove unexpectedly useful. On one occasion, when Mr X appeared to be emerging from his Napoleonic dream in some fresh direction, Honeybath rebuked Sister Agnes with authority when she seemed disposed to interfere. (But Mr X was frightened of Sister Agnes, and promptly shut up, all the same.) He gave Mr X two more sketches to play with, and when Mr X announced once more that the imperial archives would receive them, he repaid this courtesy by asking to be allowed to sign and date them on the spot. And this (before Mr X securely sat upon them) was done.

At the end of this sitting Honeybath could hardly credit what he had put on his own canvas. It was exploratory quite beyond the normal twitch of his tether. His portrait of this strange old man, undertaken as it had been in circumstances of mere indignity, was going to put him among the swells. Not among the small swells of his own time and country. With them, after all, he was pretty well on equal terms already. But among the *real* swells. It was a breathtaking thought.

He didn't sleep well that night. An artist doesn't, when verging on a manic condition. Even when he dozed, a brush was still in his hand, achieving incredible things. And the church clock – or was it stable clock? – was tiresome. He had never been able to understand what use to anybody was a contraption that went banging away like that all through the hours of darkness. The owls and bats, after all, didn't presumably seek to be told the time. Perhaps the performance was for the benefit of poachers and burglars. It was nothing but a damned nuisance to honest men.

He'd thought to relax by taking a bath not long after dinner, and in his bath he'd heard the thing strike nine. There was that flat effect on the last stroke. He heard it again in bed: at ten the penultimate stroke went wrong, and at eleven the antepenultimate. He told himself that this phenomenon reminded him of something, but he was quite unable to determine what it was. The point worried him unreasonably, and it was almost fretfully that he waited for midnight. Light, however, came to him before then. It came to him out of *The Waste Land*, the poem with which the obscurely apocalyptic voice of T S Eliot had so deliciously troubled Charles Honeybath's generation when young. In *The Waste Land* one is told something about St Mary Woolnoth, which is in Lombard Street, London, among (it is to be supposed) the bankers. It is therefore known as one of Sir Christopher Wren's City Churches, although it is in fact by Wren's pupil, Nicholas Hawksmoor. It is scarcely one of Hawksmoor's successes, since it looks like a gaol upon the roof of which some inexplicable atomic catastrophe has landed an undistinguished classical temple. But it is not this that is commemorated in the celebrated poem. It is the fact that St Mary Woolnoth keeps the hours *with a dead sound on the final stroke of nine*. In an annotation the poet assures us that there can be no mistake, since the phenomenon is one which he has often noticed.

Although in a drowsy and somewhat confused state, Honeybath didn't fall for the error that he was actually in Eliot's Unreal City, and flowing up the hill and down King William Street, now. He was deep in the country; there could be no doubt about that. It was simply that he was in contact with the effects of a similar mechanical deficiency to that commemorated in the poem. And not even precisely similar. Strictly read, *The Waste Land* asserted that only twice in the twenty-four hours – to wit when the striking of nine o'clock was in question – was the dead sound perceptible. 'The final stroke of nine' was quite unambiguous. Whereas here it was any ninth stroke that went wrong. There must be a missing tooth, or something of the kind, on some wheel or cog.

Honeybath in his muzzy state was so proud of working out this nice discrimination that he failed for some moments to reflect on its irrelevance. But there was something, he presently saw, that was very relevant indeed. Not many clocks in the south of England could be relied upon to behave in this way eight times out of twenty-four.

Set out from Paddington, plod along the line of the Great Western Railway, allow yourself (like Sir John Betjeman) to be sufficiently Summoned by Bells, and you would infallibly run to earth the residence of *Mon Empereur*, otherwise known as Mr X.

6

Several unremarkable days succeeded. Honeybath was now in a position to advance his painting in a number of regards without the presence of his sitter, and he achieved long hours of concentrated labour which once more left him without any very urgent impulse to quarrel with his situation. He had, in fact, fallen into a routine. The extent to which this was so became clear to him only when certain interruptions – not seemingly very significant interruptions – eventually came along.

One morning Mr X was wheeled into the painting-room not by Sister Agnes but by Mr Peach. It was, it appeared, Sister Agnes' day off, and Peach was standing in for her. Honeybath, of course, had never seen Peach outside his own studio, and he found himself not particularly pleased at seeing him again now. It wasn't that he regarded him as excessively sinister. He regarded Sister Agnes, indeed, although he could hardly have said why, as a good deal the more sinister of the two. But he remembered Peach as an underbred and shifty little man who was entirely tedious. He disliked having to recall that he had even accepted banknotes planted before him by the fellow. He thought, no doubt unreasonably, that so affluent an outfit as he had become entangled with could readily have substituted for Sister Agnes another perhaps grim, but at least quiet and correct, trained nurse.

Peach wasn't quiet. He insisted on inspecting the portrait, and this Honeybath regarded as an impertinence. He ventured to make comments on it, which was less an impertinence than an outrage.

'Very fine, Mr Honeybath – very fine, indeed, if the liberty to say so may be allowed me. Undoubted *gusto*, as I believe the critics say. And abundant *chiaroscuro* – almost lavish, in a manner of speaking. But perhaps the old gentleman's complexion might be toned up a little? No more than a suggestion, Mr Honeybath. Just as it is, some might think it a shade on the unhealthy side. A liver condition, perhaps. Whereas he's as hearty as can be, isn't he?' This last question was addressed not to Honeybath but to Mr X himself. It was as if Peach regarded it as a matter of good form to address only in the third person one who was unhappily of unsound mind. 'He's in as fine fettle as he has been for years, eh?'

'Hold your tongue, my good man, and let Monsieur David get on with his work.' This sharp retort by the victor of Marengo and Austerlitz was the first sign that today was not to be exactly like previous days. Sister Agnes, perhaps, had Mr X under her thumb in a way that Peach had not. Peach was uneasy with his charge. His enhanced vulgarity – he was back, you might say, to Lesson One – seemed an index of this.

But Mr X himself was uneasy too. He kept shifting restlessly in his chair, so that Honeybath knew they were in for a difficult session. He wondered whether Sister Agnes' absence had resulted in some tranquillizing pill or jab having got missed out. Of course, to have the opportunity of observing his subject in a changed mental state might well be interesting and valuable in itself. In psychological portraiture – and what other sort of portraiture was worth twopence in these days? – one had to work in depth. Ideally, layer upon layer, right down to the depths of the personality, ought all to be there. Sophisticated novels were like that in the present age. And Honeybath knew he had it in him to produce something quite as good as any sophisticated novel. It was going to be an edgy morning, all the same.

And then the cars began to arrive.

The painting-room faced north, as it ought to do. It had a single large window, from which there was quite a different view to that from Honeybath's bedroom. It wasn't at all an extensive or informative view, but Honeybath had got into the way of surveying it from time to time by way of relieving the strain of his work. There was simply a great gravel sweep, probably leading to the front door of the house, and beyond it one saw only the high wall of the garden in which he went for those tiresomely invigilated walks or toddles with Arbuthnot. There had never been the slightest sign of life or traffic on this sweep – but now first one car had arrived, and then another. Within half an hour there were almost a dozen cars parked side by side. They were rather grand cars, for the most part – quite as grand as the one in which Honeybath had himself been driven here. Executive-type cars, a car-salesman would have said.

Mr X, of course, couldn't survey this transformed scene. But it was obvious that he had been aware of each vehicle as it drove up. He was distracted, and so was Honeybath. Honeybath suddenly got a highlight grotesquely wrong. It was most confoundedly annoying.

'Is there a board meeting?' Mr X asked.

Honeybath was startled. It wasn't an expression which *Mon Empereur* could conceivably use of a council of war at which the Marshals of France gathered themselves deferentially around him. Moreover, Mr X's voice had been a new voice. And it was evident that it alerted Peach at once.

'He's got it wrong, hasn't he?' Peach had jumped up and advanced upon Mr X in a disagreeable way. 'He'd better quit that line, had he not?'

'Sit down, sir.' Mr X's pallid countenance had amazingly taken on a faint flush. 'Do you think I'm going to be spoken to in that way by a damned jumped-up clerk? Behave yourself, or a week's wages will he the end of the matter. And you can whistle for the ghost of a reference from me. You'll be tramping the streets on public assistance, or whatever the nonsense is called, within a month.'

Honeybath would have relished this odd metamorphosis but for the fact that there was something brutal about it. Here was Mr X, for a change, in some character he had once really owned, and it didn't suggest itself as at all estimable.

'Now, come to your senses,' Mr X said. He hesitated for a moment, almost as if dimly aware of the curious character of these words from his lips. 'And answer me,' he continued hectoringly. 'Is it a board meeting?'

'And what if it is?' Peach showed signs of losing grip of the situation. 'What has it got to do with you, you old lunatic? A pretty figure you'd cut at a high-level thing like that. Belt up, do you hear?'

'Take me to it at once.' Mr X was struggling, feebly and distressingly, in his chair. His voice had risen a pitch – as, indeed, Peach's had done. 'I'll have you know I know my rights in this place. I'll have you up before the Governor. I'll let no bloody screw – '

Quite suddenly, Mr X collapsed. He slumped, and a faint froth of spittle appeared on his lips. Honeybath was horrified – partly, perhaps, for the selfish reason that he didn't want to find himself painting a corpse. And he saw that Peach, having recovered himself, was about to wheel his employer, patient, captive – impossible to define the relationship – from the room.

'One moment,' Honeybath said peremptorily. 'Just what does this mean? Why is he talking about a Governor? What does he mean by a bloody screw? I insist – '

'Only another of his fancies, Mr Honeybath. Another of the poor old gentleman's imaginary lives, you might say. And a very distressing one – a very distressing one, indeed. Particularly embarrassing for the relations, sir – the family always having been so highly respectable, and lucky enough to keep clear of anything of the kind. I have very strict instructions about when it happens, Mr Honeybath. Immediate rest and quiet is what Mr X must have on these occasions. So you'll be good enough to let me pass at once. I dare say he may be sufficiently recovered to continue the sittings this afternoon. Wonderfully resilient he is, isn't he?' Again this last question was addressed directly – but scarcely in an affectionate tone – to Mr X. Mr X, however, was not in a condition to offer an opinion on the matter. He appeared to be in some sort of coma. And Peach wheeled him out.

Honeybath returned to his room. He was thoroughly upset himself, and ventured on a stiff whisky earlier in the day than usual. This might have been expected a little to lull his senses, but, in fact the effect was rather to the contrary. At least his hearing seemed to become oddly acute. Normally the great house in which he was all but immured was soundless to a point of inducing nervous distress. Now it seemed alive and breathing. He heard, or imagined he heard, purposive footfalls in long corridors, doors briskly opening and closing, voices, now and then a telephone bell, even the muted clatter of a typewriter. His solitary lunch turned up as usual, and at about the same time there was a distinguishable change in the bruit and rumour from below. The voices were louder for a time, as if among a large group of people animated talk was going on. There was a clink and rattle of cutlery and glass. The volume of sound increased. It hinted jollity, as if the wine had been going round at some informal buffet occasion. Then it ceased almost abruptly. The board – it came suddenly to Honeybath – had renewed its deliberations. Once more, there were only occasional footsteps, an opening or closing door.

Half an hour later, he returned to his painting-room. He doubted whether Mr X would indeed be trundled in again that day, but there was still plenty he could do. In the background to the figure several small areas remained to be animated without being rendered too busy, or irritating the aerial perspective. He addressed himself to one of these, but was unable quite to trust his touch. He had developed, in fact, the ghost of an intention tremor, which is a disability not comfortable for an artist to contemplate. So he gave over, and prowled the room. He peered through the window. One of the parked cars was backing out; it swung clear and drove away.

There were voices in the open air below. The party was breaking up. First one and then another figure appeared on the sweep; soon there were half a dozen or more, talking rather loudly to each other, or shouting hearty farewells. They appeared, on the whole, a burly but rather out-of-condition crowd; their heads were visible, bobbing above large circumferences of foreshortened bellies and buttocks. Honeybath could distinguish nothing of what was being said, but gained a sharp impression of the tones and accents employed. There were voices, among which he thought he distinguished Arbuthnot's, luxuriating in the purities of the Queen's English; but there were rather more voices in one degree or another unrefined. Vulgar voices, to put it broadly.

What sort of people of that kind drove around in large cars and attended mysterious conclaves in congruously large country mansions? People who managed the affairs of important football clubs? Or who promoted prize-fights at world championship level? Or who ran gaming-houses, or revivalist religious rackets, or clip-joints (whatever clip-joints were), or call-girl services? Of any one of these numberless goings-on of human life Honeybath knew, if possible, less than of another. But he did know that these men were not Royal Academicians holding a soirée, or Professors of the Exegesis of Holy Scripture in conference. It didn't even seem likely that they were the Confederation of British Industry or the Trades Union Congress intent upon marvellously mending the world. Fleetingly he wondered whether they were just plain crooks.

That evening, life returned to normal. With his dinner Honeybath was sent up a bottle of Moët et Chandon, *Dom Perignon*, 1964, and Arbuthnot came in and took a glass of it with him towards the end of the meal. Mr X, Arbuthnot said, was now quite himself again; there had been a small family gathering in the middle of the day, and the sight of all his relations had quite set the old boy up. They were a very united family, Arbuthnot said. There was nothing of which they were more aware than that dissention simply doesn't pay.

7

The portrait was completed. The brief moment had arrived – it always does – in which Honeybath saw his work for exactly what it was. The canvas by no means embodied that irradiated conception which had visited him halfway through. He was far – oh, so far! – from having achieved one of the great paintings of the world. Even so, he had never achieved anything like it before. His *Portrait of an Unknown Gentleman* would go into the histories and monographs as a signal instance of an accomplished academic painter's transcending himself.

But what was to happen to the thing? There was, of course, a sense in which its immediate fortunes didn't matter. The likelihood of its perishing unregarded, of being tossed contemptuously on some scrapheap twenty or thirty years on, was mercifully small. His mere signature on the canvas, spelling a reasonable little heap of guineas (and just conceivably a large one) in any civilized future, was an adequate assurance of that. It would be pleasant, all the same, if its existence could be made known to an informed public now. If no more than two or three eminent critics had a glimpse of it, that would be enough in itself to establish the fact that he had achieved a notable thing. Unfortunately, in view of the mania for secrecy these people had, it didn't look as if anything of the kind could be managed.

He was to leave after dinner, and on this final occasion there was again a bottle of champagne. Arbuthnot, however, didn't turn up to share it. Honeybath had no great fondness for Arbuthnot, and in general would as soon have enjoyed his room as his company. On this occasion, however, he found himself disposed to feel that a courtesy had been neglected. It was as if he had done his job, and that was that, and he could clear out and not be heard of again. It was true that on his dinner-table there had appeared a small packet which proved to contain fifty-five £20 notes, so that he was now in possession of his entire two thousand guineas. This was mollifying – but he derived no great comfort from it, all the same. What was chiefly in his mind was that he might never again set eyes on the best thing he had ever done.

The younger manservant carried his possessions to the lift. When he himself emerged on the ground floor the familiar chauffeur took charge of him, whisking him, as on that earlier occasion, straight into the limousine. They moved off at once. The briskness of this confused Honeybath's feelings. He told himself that this was escape, and that he should be nothing other than thankful for it. Like the Thane of Cawdor's guests, he was standing not on the order of his going, but going at once. He remembered the physician (also resident in Macbeth's castle) who had remarked that, were he from Dunsinane away and clear, even the hardest cash would not take him back to the place. To *this* place he was pretty sure he would never willingly return himself. He felt an odd pang on parting from it, all the same. He was leaving his masterpiece behind him.

It was already very dark. And the car was already stuffy. Several times during his immurement he had cast his mind back to his first journey, and he had convinced himself – incredible though it seemed – that some stupefying drug had been brought into play upon him. Perhaps it had been provided by the sinister Sister Agnes. As he hadn't swallowed anything, or been conscious of the slightest prick or jab, it must, he supposed, have been an anaesthetic gas. He certainly wasn't going to stand for anything of the kind this time. They hadn't emerged from the drive – there seemed to be a notably long drive – before he had picked up the intercom affair and addressed the chauffeur in a tone of the sternest command.

'I can't stand this atmosphere, my man. And I don't propose to put up with any of your damned air-conditioning, either. Be good enough simply to open one of these windows at once.'

'Certainly, sir. You have only to mention it.' The chauffeur was as smooth as his vehicle. He appeared to touch a button on the dashboard (which they no doubt called the control panel) and the window by Honeybath's left ear shot down to its full extent. 'Is that agreeable to you, sir?'

'Excellent.' The air now so freely admitted was soon going to prove uncommonly chilly, but Honeybath turned up his collar and was resolved to suffer it gladly. He would at least stay awake. So, even if he could make little of their route, he would be able to reckon just how long the journey took, and remark eventually from what direction they entered London. In a way, he oughtn't to be caring a damn. So long as he was returned to Chelsea (and not dumped into the Thames) the affair would be ending reasonably enough. But he was a little on his mettle. It would be satisfactory to collect at least one trick.

They drove for a surprisingly long time, and entirely through rural solitudes. A good deal of careful planning, Honeybath thought, must have gone to finding a seemingly endless succession of country roads which didn't traverse so much as a single identifiable hamlet. They covered at least fifty miles that way. And fifty miles represents a considerable stretch of territory in tight little England.

Something was happening to the engine. It was misfiring in a manner not at all pardonable in a car of this kind. The car began to move jerkily; to lose momentum and then pick up again. There was something wrong with the ignition, or with the feed. Suddenly all the lights went out, and Honeybath thought he could actually hear the chauffeur swear loudly as he abruptly drew to a halt. Then there was the swaying light of an electric torch, and the man had opened a door and was getting out. He came at once to Honeybath's open window.

'I'm very sorry, sir, but I'm afraid it's the alternator. It's quite shocking, the way even high-class cars are turned out of British factories these days. What kind of a foreign market can they expect?'

'What kind, indeed.' Honeybath didn't much mind about this. The whole wide world was already abominably over-crammed with cars. But he did feel impatient. 'Can you fix it yourself?'

'Oh, yes. No difficulty, sir, about a temporary repair. But it may take the best part of a quarter of an hour. Very sorry, sir – but that's how it is. Would you care for the rug, sir? A chilly night.'

Honeybath accepted the rug. He was a little assuaged by this ready solicitude. The chauffeur raised the bonnet of the car, and together with the torch more or less disappeared beneath it. There were tinkering sounds. Quite a long time passed. Honeybath fidgeted. Eventually the man reappeared.

'The alignment's been faulty from the start, sir, if you ask me. It's bound to take a bit longer than I reckoned. If another car came by, I think I'd have them take a message to the nearest garage. It could probably provide a car to run you into town. I've no doubt it's what Mr Arbuthnot would desire. He would be most upset at your being put to this inconvenience.'

'That's not a bad idea.' Rather wildly, Honeybath reflected that, once safely in a hired vehicle, he would be secure against even that remote possibility of being chucked into a river. 'Wasn't that something like a main road that we shot across a quarter of a mile back?'

'Yes, sir – and quite a lot of traffic. I wonder whether you would care to walk back yourself, and hail something. You'd have the authority, in a manner of speaking.'

'I think I will.' Honeybath was gratified at having authority attributed to him. He was even more gratified by the mere blind thought of getting away.

'I have a second torch, sir. So you needn't be blundering in the dark.' The chauffeur dived into his own part of the interior, and the second torch was produced. 'Stretch your legs, anyway,' he said benevolently.

So Honeybath set out. He hadn't walked fifty yards before being cheered by a flash of headlamps somewhere ahead of him. He could certainly stop a car. People were very decent, on the whole, about that sort of thing.

He became aware of a sound behind him. There must be another car approaching from that direction too. But the sound didn't increase. It rapidly faded. He turned round. Mr Arbuthnot's car and Mr Arbuthnot's chauffeur, together with the personal and professional effects of Charles Honeybath RA, were vanishing into distance, swallowed up by the night.

PART TWO

KEYBIRD INVESTIGATES

8

Honeybath decided to contact the police. It wasn't a necessary decision; it mayn't even have been a wise one. He was in no sense badly stuck or stranded. There really was a main road close by; and anybody prepared to stop and take him to a police station would presumably have been equally willing to take him to a garage. He had money in his pocket (an embarrassingly large amount of it, although he didn't think of this), and in no time he could have hired himself a Rolls Royce had he a mind to it. The truth is that he chose to search out the local police because he was feeling uncommonly vindictive.

He had been dismissed from his recent employment, it appeared to him, with precisely the equivalent of a mocking guffaw and a contemptuous kick in the pants. He told himself (but he was wrong in this) that there was no reason at all why those people, without the slightest risk to themselves, should not have returned him to his studio exactly as they had brought him away from it. Playing this final trick on him was a gratuitous impertinence. The fact that they had handed him the balance of his promised fee, when they could perfectly well have cheated him of it, was a consideration which somehow merely added to his sense of insult. He waved quite furiously at one or two disregarding and obviously unsuitable vehicles.

And then a police car actually came along. It wasn't an imposing affair; in fact it was no more than a small dun-coloured van. But it did have on its roof one of those reassuring revolving blue lights. It drew to a halt at once upon Honeybath's waving at it.

'Yes, sir. Can I be of any help to you?' The constable at the wheel was reassuring too. Spend a fortnight in irregular and outrageous captivity, and any policeman will probably strike you like that.

'I want to be taken to the nearest police station. I have something serious to report. Is it far away?'

'Only a couple of miles, sir, and I'm on the way there now.' The constable politely opened a door, saw Honeybath seated beside him, and drove on. 'Becoming quite chilly,' he said. He didn't seem particularly impressed or curious.

'It's to be expected at this time of year.' Honeybath had decided against immediately pouring out his story to this rather stolid-seeming officer. Come to think of it, it was rather an odd and complex story – if indeed it was a story at all. What you reported to the police were burglaries, assaults, public nuisances, stolen cars, missing persons. Honeybath didn't really have anything in these categories to complain about. Nothing at all had really happened to him – he suddenly saw – that the law would be prepared to take an interest in. He was making a fool of himself. And his only grievance was that he himself had lately been made a fool of.

But he could hardly tell this fellow that he had changed his mind, and that all he wanted was useful advice on how to get himself back to London in comfort. He sat back in the little van to consider his problem. The result was immediately alarming: nothing less than something warm and wet curling itself round his throat. He produced a yell – a half-strangled yell, because of the nature of this embrace – and managed to turn round a little in his seat. An enormous and slavering Alsatian dog was gazing at him reproachfully – clearly hurt in its mind that a demonstration of affection had been misinterpreted.

'Don't mind Radar, sir,' the constable said soothingly. 'It's only villains Radar has it in for. He won't harm *you*.'

'Radar?' Honeybath said stupidly. He had been absurdly discomposed. 'Is that dog called Radar?'

'*Called* Radar?' The constable, like the dog, seemed hurt in his mind. 'That *is* Radar.'

'I see.' Honeybath wasn't entirely clear about the distinction. 'A very good name for a police dog,' he added judicially – and perhaps with some intention of ingratiating himself with Radar as well as with Radar's handler. He saw that his nerves were bad. For some time ahead, he was going to be easily upset.

But at least the drive was quite short, and he presently found himself inside a police station. There seemed to be not much more than a single stuffy little room; it was furnished with a bench, and with a counter behind which a second officer, apparently a sergeant, was shuffling some papers in a dispirited way.

'Gentleman has a complaint,' the first policeman said. He might have been a hospital clerk propelling the next out-patient before a doctor.

'Yes, sir. Name, please?' The sergeant scarcely looked up. He sounded extremely bored. It was improbable, Honeybath thought, that an insignificant station like this was manned all night. These two fellows – not to speak of Radar – were no doubt thinking of packing up and going home. They wouldn't care for his odd recital at all. Perhaps it was just as well – and perhaps, indeed, he had better abandon the notion of delivering himself of it. He'd simply explain that there had been a hitch in transport, and ask them to whistle up something to get him home. And then he could do a little thinking as to whether he wanted to have any dealings with the police after all.

'Name, please?' the sergeant repeated. He had reached listlessly for a large diary or register, and was poising a pen over it.

'My name's Honeybath.'

'*Charles* Honeybath?' The sergeant had straightened up abruptly, and his free hand went out to grab a file from a corner of the counter.

'Certainly. Charles Honeybath.' Honeybath was impressed and pleased. The sergeant, despite appearances to the contrary, must take an informed interest in contemporary art. 'The painter,' he added. 'As you've guessed.'

'Quite so, sir.' The sergeant paused, much as if verifying his facts in the dossier now before him. When he looked up, there was something slightly devious (it might have been maintained) about the movement of his head. Could the first constable (Honeybath's rescuer, as Honeybath thought of him) have taken this for a signal or a sign? He had been standing gloomily warming himself before a small cheerlessly black stove; now he made his way casually to a position in front of the door. So did Radar. And Radar at once began to make disagreeable panting noises. It was almost as if the sagacious brute discerned a villain in the offing. 'Would you oblige me, sir,' the sergeant went on, 'by turning out your pockets?'

'What the devil do you mean?' Strange things had been said to Charles Honeybath during the past fortnight, but surely this was the most outrageous of the lot.

'Now, now – I think we understand each other very well.' The sergeant's tone had suddenly become almost benevolently indulgent. 'Just routine, wouldn't you say? Here on the counter, you remember – and you get a receipt at once. Keep your handkerchief. And any 5p bits. They're useful to get coffee out of the machine at headquarters. Or tea or cocoa, for that matter. Very comfortable they make you there, nowadays.'

'Good God, officer!' Honeybath's indignation was extreme. 'Are you taking me for some habitual criminal?'

'Now, now – no need to jump to conclusions. Just the contents of your pockets.'

It came to Honeybath that he was in the clutches of an extremely stupid man – the kind of policeman that private detectives make rings round in romances of crime. And it was almost worse than being in the clutches of extremely clever men – which he suspected to have been his case until a couple of hours before. It came to him too, and with much greater force, that the noises now being made by Radar were very horrid indeed. He turned out his pockets.

The sergeant wrote everything down, so the effect was of some fatuously conducted pencil-and-paper game. Not perhaps unnaturally, he was particularly interested in the £20 notes.

'Well, well. Well, well, well!' The sergeant's voice, as he finished counting all this highly negotiable wealth, was constrained to a note as of reluctant admiration. 'Just think of that,' he said to the constable.

'Christ!' the constable said.

'Christ!' Radar said. (Or Honeybath *thought* Radar said this. But then he was by now becoming very confused indeed.)

'And now, sir,' the sergeant said, with recovered poise and broad irony, 'I wonder whether you would just care to mention where you have been spending these last fourteen days?'

'I haven't the slightest idea.'

'That's very interesting, now. It would have been what they call magnesia, would it? Loss of memory, like?'

'Nothing of the kind. I've never suffered from amnesia – which is the word you want – in my life. I don't believe in such rubbish.' Honeybath was now shouting wildly. 'I was kidnapped. It's what I came to tell you about – and you behave like bloody fools.'

'Language, now, Mr Honeybath, language.'

'Damn language. And I shall go in person to the Home Secretary.'

'Yes, sir. It's always a wise course. So you were kidnapped?' The sergeant turned to his colleague. 'It's a story, all right,' he said admiringly. 'A deep one, he is. No wonder they're after him bald-headed.'

'I insist on telling you – ' Honeybath began.

'Well, of course, sir. If you feel you must, that is. But I'd advise you to wait till they arrive.' The sergeant had picked up a telephone. 'They'll be here within ten minutes, I'd say. And delighted to hear anything you have to offer. Smart fellows, you'll find them.'

'Who the devil are *they*?'

'Regional Crime Squad for a start, Mr Honeybath. Detective Superintendent Keybird in charge, sir. Easy name to remember, wouldn't you say? And don't you bother about their ranks and titles. Just call them all Mister, same as you've always done.'

'I've never encountered a person of that sort in my life.'

'Well, well! Now – ' But the sergeant's call had gone through. 'Honeybath,' he said briefly into the instrument. 'We've got him.'

If the rural constabulary of heaven alone knew where had got him, the Regional Crime Squad carried him off in a rapidly definable direction – straight, in fact, to the metropolis. They did this at speed. The car was a very powerful car; there was another car ululating ahead of them; he had a dim persuasion that the cavalcade closed with a third car behind. Constables on motor-bicycles performed the function of outriders; they wove in and out waving other traffic more or less into the ditch. The police were doing no more than show the flag; it is wholesome that the populace (including any criminals who may be around) should be shown the terror of the law at work. Honeybath might have been what is called a high-security felon, being whisked, through some obscure necessity, from incarceration in one corner of the country to incarceration in another. A police officer sat on each side of Honeybath. They weren't at all like the rural constables. They would have regarded bluff insult or grim silence as equally unacceptable. They offered polite conversation from time to time. This added a final touch of the bizarre to his incredible ride. And then suddenly the car had slowed beside Honeybath's bank; had drawn to a halt before the door of Honeybath's studio.

'So we've got you safely home, sir,' one of his gaolers pleasantly remarked.

Mr – or Detective Superintendent – Keybird was exceedingly civil; he was only less civil than concentrated and alert. He barely had a face; his features were commonplace in the extreme; if Honeybath instantly felt that he wanted to set up a canvas before this high-ranking pig or dick it was because of the almost unbearable intensity of his pale blue eyes. They were the kind of eyes that pretty well said *I God see you*. Honeybath recalled eccentricities, conceivably illegal, in his extreme youth, and felt for some moments very frightened indeed.

That Keybird received him, in the first instance, across the chasm added to his perturbation. Here was this appalling bloodhound from New Scotland Yard or whatever on one side of the gaping hole, and here was he – in his own studio – on the other. The studio had been bombed, or something like that. In a rational frame of mind, one would suppose that nothing more had happened than one of those more or less lethal explosions that trouble with a gas supply occasions from time to time. Or it could be one of those political things. Every now and then bits and pieces of London get blown up by persons anxious to propagate one or another enlightened reform of society. But why should the modest *atelier* of Charles Honeybath be chosen for such a demonstration? It didn't make sense.

'Mind your step, Mr Honeybath,' Keybird said. The words may, or may not, have been double edged. 'Perhaps you didn't expect that it would be quite like this?'

'I didn't expect anything. I don't know what you're talking about. I've had a tiring day, and I want to go to bed.' Honeybath quite surprised himself by the firmness with which he said this. 'I can see there's been some sort of accident. But, if you want to talk about it, I'll be obliged if you'll come back in the morning.'

'You sleep here regularly, sir?'

'No, I don't. Only from time to time, when I have a press of work on hand.'

'There's been nobody to miss you during the past fortnight?'

'I don't care a damn whether there has been or not. I just want to go to sleep. But, for what it's worth, I left a note at my flat. For the woman who comes in and tidies up.'

'So you went away of your own free will?'

'Certainly I did. It's complicated. But certainly I did.'

'I understand you to have told the police when you contacted them that you had been kidnapped. Perhaps that was just a joke?'

'It was nothing of the kind. But, for the moment, I simply decline to discuss the matter. My mind is confused.'

'Perhaps you feel it would be prudent to talk only in the presence of your solicitor? That would be perfectly in order.'

'I feel nothing of the kind. I simply want you to clear out, and to take all these men with you. Are you prepared to assert that I am under arrest? Do you hold a warrant entitling you to be on these premises without my permission?'

'Mr Honeybath, I hope you will not wish to be too legalistic about this. I am simply asking for your assistance – your immediate assistance, despite your very understandable fatigue – in view of the fact that a major crime has been mounted from your studio.'

'Mounted! What the devil do you mean?'

'The bank next door has been robbed, in one form or another, of close on half a million pounds. And the operation' – Keybird pointed to the chasm – 'began there.'

'Half a million pounds!' As if from far away, Honeybath's own voice came to him, stupidly repeating this sum. The chasm, the pit, was swimming before him. 'That's a lot of money.'

'It is indeed, sir. Worth organizing for. Worth considerable preliminary outlay here and there.'

'Yes – of course.'

What was for some time to seem to Honeybath the truth of the matter presented itself to him in a flash. It was a humiliating truth. That portrait of Mr X – the best thing he had ever done – hadn't really been wanted at all. The distinguished company in which he had been assured it was going to hang simply didn't exist. Nobody had given a damn for the thing – or was giving the thing a damn now. By this time it had probably been stuffed into some furnace in that horrible house – just to help the central heating along. The vast mortification in this stunned Honeybath. But as well as mortified he was angry. A small glow of primitive rage – to be fateful for his future – was kindling somewhere in his stupefied mind. The vanity of the artist (which can be almost as devouring as the vanity of the writer) was already at work upon him. His painting had been held at nought.

'Perhaps,' Keybird was saying, 'you had arranged to go off and work elsewhere? It would have been inconvenient for you – to have all this digging and delving and trucking and propping and steel-cutting going on under your nose as you pursued your own professional activities.'

'Arranged to–?' Unbelievingly, Honeybath picked up the operative words. 'Do I understand you to be suggesting I have been in some collusive arrangement with these robbers?'

'Not necessarily collusive, Mr Honeybath. But what may loosely be called an arrangement there certainly seems to have been.'

9

Keybird's assertion was undeniable. A moment's sober thought showed Honeybath that something which must be called an 'arrangement' *had* existed between himself on the one hand and the atrocious Arbuthnot and his associates on the other. Moreover he realized, with dawning misgiving, that he had an uncommonly tall story to tell.

But at least his studio was now less like a movie set for some gangster film. Keybird's assistants had withdrawn, whether for good or for a time. Faint noises coming through the tunnel (for there was, of course, a tunnel as well as a chasm) suggested that criminal investigation was still going forward in the bank. This prompted Honeybath to a question.

'Would you mind telling me, Mr Keybird, just when this happened?'

'Of course not.' Keybird gave a faint smile which Honeybath didn't at all like. It suggested awareness of the possibility – to put it no stronger than that – that Honeybath had produced a query to which he already knew the answer. Honeybath vaguely saw that there was, so to speak, no malice in this. It was Keybird's business to harbour every possible sort of suspicion and to neglect no opportunity of rattling and panicking pretty well everybody he had to deal with. The obligation wasn't calculated to conduce to tranquil and companionable chat. 'Of course not,' Keybird repeated. 'The actual robbery happened in the small hours of this morning.'

'Then they didn't lose all that time in releasing me.'

'Ah!' The professional smile had appeared again on Keybird's featureless face. It didn't extend to those eyes. 'The kidnapping – of course. Did they – whoever they are, and that's what I have to find out – did they give you all that money, Mr Honeybath, in return for the inconvenience they'd put you to? Or do you always carry around something over a thousand pounds in cash?'

'Of course I don't.' Honeybath was annoyed. 'And I take you to be referring to the bundle of £20 notes those constables impounded in what was an uncommonly high-handed manner.'

'Yes, I am. And it was high-handed. Irregular, in fact. I wouldn't dispute it for a moment. Still, Mr Honeybath, it looks as if you and I have more serious things to think about.'

'That seems to be perfectly true.' Honeybath considered it politic to respond at once to this note of reason.

'Now, when they picked you up – '

'Picked me up?' Honeybath was offended again.

'Ah, not in that sense. I don't suggest for a moment that they ran you to earth. One of them simply picked you up in a patrol car. You had put yourself in his way.'

'You can call it that, if you like.' Honeybath again didn't much care for Keybird's command of ambiguity. 'As for the money, there was more of it, as a matter of fact. May I ask whether you have judged yourself empowered to rifle my private possessions in this studio?'

'We have done nothing not, in our judgement, directly necessary to the business of elucidating the crime.' Keybird said this quite stiffly.

'That drawer in the desk, for instance.' Honeybath pointed. 'Has it been broken open by the robbers? Or have you picked the lock?'

'Most certainly not. It's untouched, so far as I can see.'

'Then here is the key.' Honeybath walked over to the chimneypiece and fished behind a clock. 'Be so good as to open the drawer and find what you can in it. Be careful, though. Fingerprints, and so forth.'

'Thank you.' Keybird didn't seem amused by this kindly piece of advice. 'A further thousand pounds,' he said presently.

'Quite so. And, as your rural colleagues would say: well, well, well. It was too late to get it into the bank, of course, that day a fortnight ago. Which means, come to think of it, that the thieves' haul was diminished by that amount. A gratifying thought, Mr Keybird.'

'Very true, sir.' Keybird's smile was again not reassuring. Perhaps he felt things were going well when he edged people into turning a bit cocky. Honeybath decided to stick to a cautious note. 'So it appears,' Keybird went on, 'that the total may be called two thousand guineas. They were prepared to go to that figure as an inducement to clear out. Imaginative, wouldn't you say?'

'I don't know what you mean by imaginative. The sum is certainly in excess of my usual fee.'

'For smoothing the way of bank robbers?' It was impossible to be certain whether this from Keybird was an outrage or a joke. Honeybath decided to ignore it.

'In fact,' he said, 'it is nearly double my usual fee. I felt entitled to push up the figure, simply because the proposal was such an extraordinary one.'

'A proposal made to you professionally as a portrait-painter?'

'Of course. And by a man calling himself Peach, and representing himself as a rather mysterious agent or go-between. He handed over just under half of the stipulated sum, there and then. You've just removed it from that drawer.'

'I see. You are quite right that it will interest the fingerprint people. And that reminds me to give you a receipt.' Keybird produced a small, official-looking form and scribbled on it. He thus owned, Honeybath thought, to the same book of rules as the rural sergeant. Then he paused and gazed at Honeybath in a brooding sort of way. It was hard not to feel that he was trying to make up his mind as to whether the cock-and-bull story this rascally artist would put up could be the least worth listening to. 'Mr Honeybath,' he then said politely, 'I shall be most grateful if you can provide me – more or less as a sustained narrative – with whatever information you feel may be useful.'

'Very well – and I'll begin at the beginning.' Honeybath checked himself. 'But – do you know? – I won't. I'll begin, as long as I remember it, with what strikes me as the oddest part of the whole affair. The place, so to speak, where the emphasis should lie.'

'A sensible plan, sir.'

'It's about the money. What you found in that drawer, they *had* to pay. There would have been no deal without it. But the second instalment – what was taken off me in that confounded country police station – they paid me, under no compulsion at all, that I can see, just before chucking me out.'

'Chucking you out?'

'It came to that. I was driven away from a totally unknown house and locality, tricked into getting out of the car, and then simply left by the roadside. And yet I was given the balance of my fee. Don't you think that odd?'

'A little confusing, no doubt.' Keybird was looking hard at Honeybath. 'Honour among thieves, perhaps?' Keybird smiled again. 'But, of course, I express that badly. And now, sir, your story. By the way, I have a tape recorder here. You won't mind if I switch it on?'

'Not in the least.' It came to Honeybath as a sudden and wonderful thing that he had nothing but truth to tell. It was possibly going to be rather dull for Keybird, whose *métier* was so clearly catching out liars. But he suspected that, to date, the Crime Squad or whatever it was called hadn't made much progress with their investigation. He was their substantial hope. And he'd do his best for them. After all, running the robbers to earth appeared to offer the only possible chance of recovering *The Portrait of an Unknown Gentleman.*

Half an hour later Keybird switched off the tape recorder.

'What first strikes me about your story,' he said easily, 'is that it hangs together quite well.'

'Thank you very much. But of course it may have been carefully rehearsed, may it not? Don't be taken in, Mr Keybird, or in too much of a hurry.'

'That's a fair warning, would you say?' Keybird had received this resentful and sarcastic speech as a mild whimsy. 'On the other hand, it doesn't ring a bell.'

'Just what do you mean by that?'

'Well, here's a large-scale robbery – not twenty yards from where you and I are sitting now. *That* rings a bell, only a bell with a lesser *timbre*, so to speak.' Keybird paused on this enigmatic remark. 'I'll tell you what quite often happens. A gang of burglars – for that's what they are – scouts around until they find a bank, or some such promising prospect, next door to an uninhabited house or an untenanted shop. They gain entrance to house or shop unobtrusively, and then they go to work. In some respects the tunnelling technique is child's play. You'd scarcely believe it, but half the banks in London have strong rooms or the like almost completely vulnerable from down below. Such folly's enough to break a man's heart, trust me.' Keybird made one of his pauses on this sudden human note. 'What is tricky, is the time factor. Tunnelling and boring, avoiding pipes and cables, shoring up weight-bearing areas, and all the rest of it: these things can't be done in a hurry. Then again, really worthwhile targets with empty premises next door aren't to be found in every street. So there's a second technique. You actually take on a tenancy, and boldly appear to be setting up a new business, or moving into a new house. Very advantageous that can be, in some ways. You can move in a whole gang of navvies, and pretty well demolish what you please in full view of the world, and have the whole job finished before local authorities and the like begin to think of inquiring about permits and licences and planning permissions and the rest of it. Keep a line of pantechnicons in the street, if you care to. Slackness all round, you know. Heartbreak again. Ours can be an uphill job.'

'I sympathize with you,' Honeybath said.

'I'm much obliged to you, I'm sure.' Keybird's smile came again. 'But there's a third technique. You do a deal with some seedy little man, known to be hard up, and hopefully none too scrupulous, whose shop or whatever – '

'Whose studio, for instance.'

'Why, yes.' Keybird appeared innocently surprised. 'A studio it might be. And you provide him with a colourable excuse for making himself scarce – say taking a fortnight at the sea to visit his old auntie.

Of course the fellow's accepting a certain risk. Eventually, awkward questions will be asked. So you have to make it well worth his while.'

'Two thousand guineas.'

'Well, no.' Keybird was at his easiest. 'Precisely *not* that. Not money of that order at all. So that's where any bell of this sort doesn't exactly ring true. But another thing. You mustn't mistake me. These chaps who conveniently take themselves off are sometimes quite honest. Only, perhaps, a bit thick.'

'Do I understand, Mr Keybird, that you're prepared to be rather charitable, and lump me in with the thickies?' Honeybath thought his employment of this demotic idiom rather neat.

'Well, sir, the simplest reading of this affair is to accept it as more or less in that area. They got you away on this fool's errand of a portrait commission. Only, the scale of the operation rather baffles me. This great house, and all that affluence, and parade of what you might call pomp and circumstance. I recognize that you're a big man in your line, and that something fairly impressive – imposing, even – would have to be laid on. Still, what you describe remains a bit steep. And another thing. This Peach: was he a gentleman?'

'No.'

'But the man calling himself Arbuthnot?'

'Yes. Decidedly yes.'

'And the madman, or pretended madman, that they called Mr X, and who liked to be called *Mon Empereur*: what about him?'

'Well, yes. And then some of the men I told you I heard and glimpsed as they left their meeting. They weren't what I'd myself think of as convincing big-time East End crooks.'

'Then it grows more and more puzzling. I know of more than one gang that could mount a robbery like this. But not with that kind of background or hinterland. It makes me feel we have a long way to go.'

There was a silence. Honeybath no longer felt he simply wanted to tumble into bed. But he did feel he wanted a drink.

'There ought to be some whisky around,' he said. 'Except that I've been told burglars commonly polish off anything of the kind. Do you mind if I look?'

'Far from it, sir.'

Whisky proved, in fact, to be available.

'Will you join me, Mr Keybird?' Honeybath asked. He had a notion that even the higher ranks of the police were obliged austerely to decline such refreshment when on the job.

'That's very kind of you. Neat.'

They drank. Honeybath reflected that the last man with whom he had indulged in such compotation had been the treacherous Mr Basil Arbuthnot. He wasn't altogether clear that Detective Superintendent Keybird need be beyond certain treacheries himself. One felt him to be not at his least dangerous, certainly, when he was being most amiable.

'A long way to go?' he said. 'You can track down that house, I suppose.'

'And find an empty shell.' There was a hint of what Honeybath felt to be the dogmatic in this reply. 'It remains important, of course.'

'If my story isn't moonshine, and the place does really exist.'

'But I think we have to begin at this end.' Keybird had ignored the consideration just advanced. 'That's how we'll recover all that money.'

What Honeybath wanted to recover was his picture. But he didn't advance this fact. And now Keybird went off at a tangent.

'Talking of money, sir. Has it occurred to you to wonder about the present legal ownership of that two thousand guineas?'

'No, it has not.' This was an honest reply. 'It hasn't entered my head. Only I'm very sure that *I* don't own it.'

'The point could be a tricky one.' Keybird appeared genuinely interested. 'Wouldn't you say that, whatever its source, it has come to you as a return upon the legitimate exercise of your professional skill?'

'Of course it has – in a sense. But it is corrupt money, passed in the prosecution of fraud and crime. I should hope for legal opinion to the effect that the bargain is therefore void. What remains my property, therefore, is the portrait.' Honeybath had got this out, after all.

'It's an interesting point of view.' Keybird was looking at Honeybath with a fresh curiosity. 'It was a success, your portrait of Mr X?'

'In my judgement, decidedly yes.'

'Even although executed in what must have been very taxing circumstances?'

'Certainly, Mr Keybird. These things can be quite as mysterious as any bank robbery. And I want to recover my portrait.'

'Yes, of course. Most natural, I'm sure.'

Charles Honeybath was offended, for he had detected a perfunctory note in this response. It was a moment from which, although neither man was aware of it, momentous consequences were to proceed.

One of these, indeed, arose before the night was out. It didn't seem possible to sleep in the studio. There was that uncomfortably gaping hole, for one thing; and for another, the whole place (which consisted only of one big room and two little ones) appeared to have been pretty well taken over by the police. In this matter Honeybath simply didn't know what his rights were. The assumption seemed to be that, as a law-abiding citizen and loyal subject, it was up to him to put up with whatever came along. But at least the police couldn't camp in his flat, which clearly had nothing to do with the case, and he allowed himself, gratefully enough, to be transported there in the same car that had brought him back to London.

It was in the last half-minute of this short drive that he recalled a curious fact. He had given Keybird a very full account of his adventures and misadventures over the past fortnight, and without the slightest consciousness of holding anything back. But he *had* held something back. When he had said to Keybird 'You can track down that house, I suppose', he had failed to add just how Keybird could start in on the job. This, he now saw, had been because Keybird had immediately suggested a certain lack of interest in that aspect of his case, or at least a sense that it was less pressing than other matters.

But wasn't it almost certain that, if Keybird had been told about the train saying *Swansea* and the clock that habitually went wrong on the ninth stroke of an hour, vigorous investigation would be set going at once? And Keybird had given a very positive impression that in affairs of this sort time was a factor of enormous importance: you got somewhere before the trail went cold, or perhaps you didn't get anywhere at all.

He ought to ask that the car be turned round, so that he could make his way back to Detective Superintendent Keybird at once. Or at least he ought to communicate this significant recollection of his to the subordinate officer who was now acting as a sort of escort.

But Charles Honeybath did neither of these things. Quite unaccountably, he sat tight and kept his mouth shut. Yet even so, and at one o'clock in the morning, his bedside telephone reproached him. He could pick it up and dial 999. He had always owned a childish ambition to have some legitimate occasion to do that. He could dial 999, explain himself, and then – no doubt by some complex piece of radio technology – speak to Keybird direct.

It is conceivable that Honeybath was about to stretch out his hand and fulfil this intention when, instead, he fell fast asleep.

10

Two letters arrived for Honeybath by the first post on the following morning. They had been directed not to his studio (which was the address he provided in *Who's Who*) but to the flat because both were from familiar acquaintances. But both were about professional matters. They conveyed requests, most agreeably expressed, for the arranging of portrait commissions. The Governors of a famous public school wanted him to paint the retiring Warden, and an equally famous City livery company, the Honourable Guild of Higglers and Tranters, besought him to perform the same service for their Master. It was at once evident to Honeybath that the recent hiccup in the pipeline which had panicked him into accepting the proposal of the wretched Peach had constituted an entirely false alarm. He was still in the swim, after all.

But he ought to fix up the preliminaries for both these jobs right away. It was a well-known point of etiquette that one did this. Like a top consultant physician approached on behalf of an adequately affluent sufferer, you offered to get things moving within the next couple of days.

Yet just what was his position studio-wise? There was that great hole in the floor, and the whole place was in the mess one would expect after tons and tons of earth and rubble have been shovelled around. And the police might be proposing to go on mucking about happily for days or even weeks. He hadn't so much as gathered whether his own mere presence would be treated as an intrusion. Fortunately the head Higgler and Tranter was a baronet, an

Alderman of the City of London, and a number of other things equally august. Dropping his name would probably occasion quite an impact. Hadn't Honeybath himself, moreover, been to prep school with nobody less than the Prime Minister? Honeybath saw that the inherent modesty of his nature and demeanour had been in danger of letting him down. He'd go straight back to the studio and, if necessary, chuck his weight around a little. For the moment, at least, any sense of being a suspected pensioner and confederate of atrocious criminals blessedly departed from him. So he substituted for his accustomed artistically ample and flowing neckwear a faded old school tie (it was a pity prep schools don't much go in for old school ties) and sallied out into London. It was a delightful morning and he didn't take a taxi – although with a further £2,520 virtually on the books he could well have afforded to do so. The exercise of walking put him in mind of the fact that he was running a little short of shoes. He called in at his bootmaker's and gave instructions that the fashioning of a couple of pairs should be put in hand forthwith.

The front door of the studio stood open, a circumstance no doubt regularized by the presence of a constable standing guard before it. As he approached, two men emerged staggering under what appeared to be a crate or portmanteau constructed out of plate armour. They were followed by another man carrying an outsize camera. Perhaps this was a terminal stage in the purely local investigation.

'Mr Keybird's compliments, sir.' The constable had stepped briskly forward. 'He's in the bank, and would be obliged if you could call on him.'

'Ah, yes.' Honeybath was resolved to be firm. 'Presently, then. I must just look into one or two things in the studio first.'

'And the Assistant Commissioner, sir. "C" Department, of course.'

'What the deuce is that?'

'Criminal Investigation, sir.' The constable had stared at such ignorance. 'And Commander Berry too, I believe.'

'And who may Commander Berry be? Salvation Army?' Honeybath at once rather regretted this witticism, which might have been described as not quite on.

'National Co-ordinator, Regional Crime Squads, seconded to Home Office, sir.'

Honeybath decided that it would be civil, and indeed politic, to succumb gracefully to all this top brass.

'Very well,' he said. 'I'll go in at once.'

At least he didn't find a kind of tribunal of inquisitors. The Assistant Commissioner's job turned out to be the uttering of expressions of polite if formal concern. He shook hands and went away, rather with the air of a man who has another precisely similar assignment next on his list. The Commander, although he stayed put, remained respectfully standing until it pleased Honeybath to sit down. The Metropolitan Police Office, it seemed, had decided to lay on a red-carpet turn. Only Keybird remained distinguishably his old self.

'Mr Honeybath,' the man who co-ordinated things said, 'we have been very much hoping to vacate your studio by midday, but it now looks as if it won't be before late afternoon. Can you bear with us so long?'

'Oh, most certainly. That seems entirely reasonable.' Honeybath was much relieved. 'You must have a great deal to see to,' he added vaguely.

'Well, of course, we have to try to see to that floor. I'm afraid that permanent repair can't begin just yet. But something which I trust will be not too inconvenient can certainly be fixed up fairly soon.'

'That will be excellent.' Honeybath paused on this, and then ventured on a tentative note of jollity. 'Just so long as I can't fall into the cellarage.'

'Quite so. Mr Keybird is going to arrange something at once. But you are quite right that there is a certain press of technical investigation. This man who called himself Peach, you see. It was only last night that we heard of him as coming to your studio, was it not? And that means a fresh sniff around.'

'I see.' Honeybath wasn't sure that he did quite see. 'You think he may have left useful traces of his presence?'

'Most certainly he did. Theoretically speaking, it's impossible for any man to come and go anywhere without leaving the next best thing to his signature behind him. Only, of course, theory and practice are not always the same thing.'

'I'd suppose not.'

'But, in this case, we do quite certainly know of something our wanted man left behind him. And he is our wanted man. I can't emphasize that too much. And my colleague Mr Keybird agrees with me.'

'Definitely,' Keybird said – distinguishably on his dogmatic note. 'Frankly, there's nothing else to go on. Or not yet.'

'I'd have thought' – Honeybath spoke from an obscure sense that he and his adventures were again being undervalued in this appreciation of the matter – 'I'd have thought that my Mr X, and Arbuthnot –'

'Yes, indeed. We shall have to come to all that. But it is certainly Peach we must go after first.' The co-ordinating character got to his feet. It was plain that he had turned up simply to lend weight to this contention. 'And I'm off on the job now. It's most satisfactory that you and Mr Keybird understand each other so well. There's a great deal in hitting it off in situations like this. But, of course, I do myself hope to see you again.'

With these bland remarks Commander Berry departed, although not without first gravely shaking hands. Honeybath watched him go in silence, and then looked around him. The room was familiar; it was his bank manager's office. He wondered what had happened to the manager – and indeed to all the branch's staff and all the branch's other customers. The robbers had presumably cleared out cash, securities, safe-deposit stuff, everything. There must be the devil of a mess to sort out. But all that was not of the first relevance at the moment. He turned to Keybird.

'Your colleague said something that puzzled me a good deal. It was something to the effect that Peach had, to your positive knowledge, left something behind him. Of course he left those banknotes. Was the reference to that?'

'Well, no – although they are certainly important. Keybird paused for a moment, rather as if hesitating before something delicate. 'You know about the identikit technique, Mr Honeybath?'

'Fudging up something said to resemble a wanted man, on the basis of people's descriptions of him? Certainly. I can't say I've ever thought much of them. Tailor's dummies are a lot more individual and expressive.'

'I'd hesitate, sir, to deny an element of truth in that.' Keybird again hesitated after this judicious concession. 'But here we have a very special factor indeed. What Peach has left behind him is his own likeness inside the head, so to speak, of the most accomplished portrait-painter in England. I hope it isn't a liberty to express the fact that way.'

If Honeybath was disconcerted it was perhaps because Keybird had here dropped into something very like the idiom of Peach himself. But he also, if rather unaccountably, took alarm at what was coming. For of just what was coming, he hadn't the slightest doubt.

'Do you think you could sketch him for us, sir? I'm aware that it is quite something to ask.'

Honeybath wondered how a policeman was aware of this. But the fact was certainly true. There are purposes to which one doesn't bend one's art without misgiving. And thief-catching was one of them. It would be like painting something to advertise a detergent or a bed-time drink. He had, it was true, every reason to wish Peach and all his company put well and truly inside. They had exploited him, and in the end (he still felt) they had gratuitously mocked him as well. Even that second payment had been a mockery. But he still didn't want to draw Peach for the police.

'Very well,' he said. 'I'll try.' A moment's thought had shown him that he couldn't really decline. 'And it won't be all that hard. In fact, Mr Keybird, I can pretty well promise to sketch him with tolerable fidelity full-face, half-face, in profile, or upside down.' Honeybath paused for appropriate signs of merriment from Keybird. 'But it will take me the better part of the day. You may find that odd. But one works towards a likeness, you know, by quite humble trial and error. And when one's subject is a memory – '

'Quite so, sir. And could you make a start on it here?' Having gained his point, Keybird wasn't for wasting time. 'The materials are available in your studio?'

'Of course they are. But it seems to me – '

'It's the villain's Achilles heel, sir. The one thing he didn't think of. If Peach is known to a single police officer in the kingdom, we'll establish his identity within twenty-four hours of your playing your part, as one may say.'

'Wouldn't the same apply – '

'He can't have been disguised to any significant extent? An eye like yours would instantly have been aware of anything like that?'

'I'm pretty confident it would.'

'Then we've as good as got him. And he's the key to the whole affair. Peach has a familiar smell, sir. And there's nothing other than run-of-the-mill about this bank robbery. It doesn't take us out of our depth.'

'And perhaps Arbuthnot, and Mr X, and that house, and that board meeting *do* do that?'

For the first time in their acquaintance, Honeybath had the pleasure of seeing Detective Superintendent Keybird halted in his stride. But his response was that of an honest man.

'Well, sir, yes – in a way. But first things first.'

11

It was only when Honeybath took a first serious glance at Peach – at Peach, that is, as Peach existed for Honeybath's inward eye – that a certain element of difficulty in fulfilling his new and odd commission revealed itself. He could see Peach perfectly. Yet Peach, thus viewed, was uncommonly like one of those identikit dummies that Honeybath had made fun of. Peach was (and Honeybath now recalled this as having been his earliest impression) one of nature's faceless men. He suggested himself as the very type of the obscure little clerk who, just because he sits on a particular stool among innumerable other obscure little clerks in some government or municipal office, can suddenly assume enormous nuisance-value in one's entirely private affairs.

For a brief space, Honeybath's first sketch from memory pleased him very much. Then he realized that his satisfaction was a malicious satisfaction, and that what he had produced was a caricature of Peach. It was possible to imagine circumstances in which it would be precisely this that was useful. Accentuation and enhancement were probably what the genuine identikit people at New Scotland Yard went after. If you were drawing a pig in order to assist visiting Martians to be quite positive that their first real pig *was* a pig, you would make your pictured pig just as piggy as you could manage. But this wasn't Charles Honeybath's notion of portraiture. That notion was a very serious one. You didn't get at the essence of a man – his quiddity, whatness, or whatever – through clever travesty. You got at it through and beyond absolute fidelity to what your visual faculty reported to you. Being incapable of violating this rule, he tore up the paper tainted by a personal dislike and started again.

In the issue, he worked all day – and policemen brought him, not once but twice, sandwiches and a half pint of bitter from the neighbouring pub. He worked with as much concentration as if he had been summoned to Number 10 Downing Street to limn his old schoolfellow, or even to Buckingham Palace itself. He had boasted foolishly to Keybird (presumably a complete Philistine) of what he could with practised facility achieve. He sweated this vainglory out of himself now. When Keybird returned to the bank at nine o'clock that night (doubtless from a refection of chops and tomato sauce) Honeybath had two sketches which he could show. Keybird took one glance at them, and instantly made as if to speak. Then he checked himself, and engaged in what appeared to be a steadying walk round Honeybath's bank manager's colourless room.

'Glory, glory!' Keybird then said.

These were surprising words. Honeybath still felt a certain antipathy towards Keybird; the man had been too abrupt with him in pursuance of his own vision of the affair. And he didn't now suppose it to be a hitherto unsuspected connoisseurship lurking in him that had prompted the exclamation. Had it been educed, nevertheless, from a committee consisting of Lord Clark and the ghosts of the late Bernard Berenson, Clive Bell and Roger Fry, he could scarcely have felt more overwhelmed for the moment. And it was for no better reason – so strange are the vagaries of the human heart – than that he had at length, in some mysterious fashion, gained merit with this common thief-catcher.

'Do you mean,' he asked, 'that it's at all likely to answer your purposes?'

'*Likely* to? Good God, sir, it's the whole thing! This is Crumble. Sammy Crumble himself. It couldn't be anybody else. What a fool he was to get himself under such an eye as yours! An utterly nondescript type – and I suppose he's come to gamble on the fact.'

'Peach is really somebody called Crumble, who is already known to the police?'

'Certainly he is. And all we have to do now is to pick him up.'

'Which is an entirely easy task?' Honeybath, although still a little overcome by the unexpected degree of his success, managed to import a mild scepticism into this inquiry.

'Easy? Why – ' Keybird checked himself in what was clearly to have been a brusque retort. 'Look, sir, have you a few hours to spare?'

'Certainly I have.'

'And you wouldn't mind cutting short another night's sleep?'

'Not in the least.'

'Then I'll show you.'

It had been designed, Honeybath was later to conclude, as a reward for good conduct, as the kind of treat given to a child who has been unexpectedly well-behaved and helpful. At the time, however, it was his thought that he was being kept an eye on. He hadn't quite recovered from being a suspected criminal. Perhaps he was still a suspected criminal. It was this that had made him – by way of showing the flag – so roundly declare that, even at the end of a day's stretching and unusual professional labour, he was fit for anything that was on. And it was thus that he came to spend a long night at the very heart of the search for Sammy Crumble.

It was an absurd name. It was even more absurd to be called Crumble than to be called Peach. Perhaps the respectable and disagreeable confidential person who had lured him into his adventure was no more a Crumble than a Peach; perhaps Crumble was merely the particular alias under which one who was really a Smith or a Brown happened to be known to the police. Not that it mattered very much. Smith or Brown or Peach or Crumble, Scotland Yard was sure that they could get him.

There was nothing particularly spectacular about the start of the operation. Keybird picked up the bank manager's telephone, dialled a number, asked for an extension, and then said 'Keybird, locations, priority Crumble S'. He listened for a moment, said 'Confirm Crumble S' and put the instrument down again.

'That will take half an hour,' he remarked apologetically to Honeybath. 'So shall we just check up on the day's work here?'

Honeybath had always vaguely supposed that his bank – this particular Chelsea branch of it, that was to say – must extend in dimensions not immediately apparent to a customer. It did so, he now discovered, in the main on a subterranean level. There was no ramification beneath his studio, since that possessed its own cellarage. But this cellarage had long since been boarded over and sealed off from the studio in the interest of housing some Tartarean electrical device the existence of which Honeybath had known nothing about. Here was the reason for the thieves having had to break through his floor. They had then, working in a constricted space, been obliged to dig down a further six feet, and so arrive at a level below those basement regions of the bank which spread extensively at the rear of the premises. Even then, there had still been much tunnelling to do, since there were four consecutive strong-rooms which could be broken into only from below. The entire operation, it seemed to Honeybath, must have been almost as highly organized as the operation going forward in the same region now.

For these industrious persons were certainly not bank staff. Nor were they – although it was what their white overalls and caps suggested – a high-powered research unit in a hospital. Perhaps they should be called forensic scientists, although it was simpler to think of them just as a new sort of policemen on the job. The evidences of what they were up against stood ranged all around them: two cavernous safes agape through doors so massive as to suggest the interior of an obsolete battleship, and which were probably equally obsolete themselves; row upon row of steel safe-deposit boxes every one of which had been cut open with the identical ruthless efficiency. On an otherwise empty table stood a small, neat pile of £5 notes. Honeybath supposed this to represent the total booty recovered so far. Or perhaps it had been deliberately left there by the thieves as an ironically conceived *pourboire* for all these toiling detectives.

'Are these fellows,' Honeybath asked, 'hunting for that signature?'

'Signature?' Keybird seemed at sea.

'I think one of your colleagues said that nobody can be physically present in a given place without leaving – '

'Ah, yes! Well, that's certainly what's going forward. And you notice that they pretty well bring their own mobile labs with them. Much more efficient than caning off samples of everything under the sun to our headquarters.'

'And what sort of form is the signature likely to take? Cigarette-ends disclosing the presence of rare tobaccos?'

'Not exactly.' Keybird laughed genially, as if in high good humour. 'I'm afraid fiction has made them rather chary of dropping anything of that kind. But smoke, now, is another matter. You wouldn't believe it, but many of them chain-smoke while on the job. The atmosphere can end up like cotton wool; you collect the stuff, shove it in a bottle or straight into a test-tube, and apply a technique of micro-analysis. Most informative at times that can be. Then again, the heat built up by their apparatus is tremendous, and they sweat like pigs. Swab themselves down, often, with a bit of cotton waste, and then chuck it away. A mistake – as are some other not very refined personal habits. Human secretions and excretions – '

'Most interesting,' Honeybath said. He could only conjecture that this fantastic talk was designed to make a fool of him. 'But I'd suppose other forms of investigation to be more promising. Do particular gangs going after this sort of thing have their regular and identifiable techniques?'

'Good question.' It was to be presumed that Detective Superintendent Keybird was in the habit of conducting seminars at police colleges. 'They certainly do, although they're smart enough to try to obliterate the traces of it. But their equipment is a limiting factor. They can't always be replacing it, and close analysis can get us quite some way. The kind of tool that cut into those boxes' – and Keybird pointed to the wall – 'well, we are often able to say where it was manufactured, to whom it was first sold, and on what occasion it was first employed on a job like this. Wonderful, wouldn't you say?'

'Oh, undoubtedly. But has any progress actually yet been achieved by these methods in this particular case?' It seemed to Honeybath that this was a fair question.

'Well, no – you have to give them time. Or they would have to be given time if I wasn't enjoying the good fortune of your co-operation, sir.' Keybird lowered his voice. 'So let's leave them to it,' he murmured. 'We've better things to do than hang around a bunch of boffins.'

This unexpected remark gratified Honeybath as much as it surprised him. Art, he felt, was carrying the day over science. His production of an identifiable Sammy Crumble had seen to that.

They drove through London – not, this time, to the accompaniment of any wailing of sirens, but making a fair speed, all the same. Within ten minutes they had reached Whitehall and the unobtrusive turn off Whitehall up which all well-informed tourists glance with quite as much interest as, a little farther north, they glance in the other direction up Downing Street. Honeybath couldn't recall having been at school with the Chief Commissioner of Metropolitan Police. But he had no doubt that, if he met the chap, they would prove to be approximately out of the same stable. So Honeybath (unlike some visitors) felt tolerably comfortable as he was driven into New Scotland Yard. It was so pervasively lit up that he wondered whether any of its inhabitants ever went home for the night. But probably they worked in shifts. There seemed to be a great many policemen in the world. There had been any number of them in that single small bank.

'We'll go right up,' Keybird said – and added mysteriously: 'It ought to be mounted by now.'

More policemen – and policewomen too. They sat in rows before switchboards in an enormous room, and as Honeybath was led past he could hear them saying into microphones things like 'Over' and 'Message timed at twenty-two hours twenty'. In fact it was so like something on television that a dispassionate spectator would have had to pronounce the spectacle somewhat banal in effect. But Honeybath was not exactly in the condition of such a spectator. He had recently been through strange and unnerving experiences, in the course of which he would on several occasions have been very glad to know that even the humblest officer of the law was at his call in case of need. Now he had been invited, through some caprice, as it seemed, of Detective Superintendent Keybird, to participate in what he realized was to be a man-hunt. His presence, it was true, could not be other than slightly otiose; he was to be like one of those devoted but dismounted persons who pant after a pack of foxhounds on foot, or stand peering over hedges in the hope of some distant prospect of a kill. But here he was, and he felt the first excitement of the chase.

There was another room. It was smaller, but still very large. It was also lofty – so lofty that it must have been almost a cube. Little furniture was visible: not much more than a table and a few upright chairs facing a huge and seemingly blank wall, hovering in shadow beyond some source of subdued light. But as Honeybath and his formidable *cicerone* entered, the wall itself lit up. What was revealed as occupying its whole extent was a map of London. This had the appearance of being etched upon a single sheet of glass or of some glass-like substance. Keybird motioned his guest to a chair, and himself sat down before the table. He gathered writing-materials to his hand.

'Begin, please,' Keybird said quietly and apparently to nobody in particular. And to Honeybath he said: 'Computerized stuff, this. But it's really very simple. Our friend's known contacts. And then *their* known contacts, sifted and selected in the light of certain obvious criteria. Not useful to have half London winking at us from the start.'

On the map a tiny light flashed on. It did, in fact, wink or blink – but this seemingly only to announce its own arrival with a kind of bow. Almost at once it settled down to a small bright glow.

'Bethnal Green,' a matter-of-fact (if somewhat Staff College) voice said somewhere in air – and gave an address and a National Grid reading. 'Crumble's father, pawnbroker, one unsuccessful prosecution for receiving 1967, one unsuccessful prosecution for dishonest handling 1968, still therefore in business 1973.'

'The stupid old machine begins with next of kin,' Keybird murmured indulgently. 'I'll bet it would obstinately go on doing so, even if it weren't programmed that way. They develop a will of their own you know. But Sammy won't be *there* just at the moment – not even if he believes he's safe as houses. Do you know what the next will be? An old auntie, if I know anything about it. Wager you a bottle of whisky.'

'Done,' Honeybath said rashly.

'Bethnal Green.' The voice gave an address again. 'Sara Crumble, aunt, National Retirement Pension and Supplementary Benefit.'

'Superannuated whore,' Keybird said comfortably but on a frankly speculative note. 'Being supported through a dishonourable old age by a grateful nation.'

'Good luck to her.' Honeybath became aware that he was capable of a certain intermittent liking for Keybird. 'Don't you think he may be with auntie?'

'No, I don't.' Keybird paused, and a third light blinked into view. 'Hullo, Hampstead! Switch to high life. Perhaps we'll take a run out to Hampstead.'

'Geoffrey de Bailhache,' the voice was saying. 'Known to the police since 1953, knighted 1960 – '

'Good God!' Honeybath exclaimed. 'I've painted him.'

'Be quiet,' Keybird said – quite politely. He was making a note. 'Now, what's this? Ah, back to Whitechapel. Nicer people, on the whole. But not invariably respecters of the law. I expect it's Finnegan. And so it is. Goes round with his pals in three pink Mercedeses. Remarkable chap.'

This weird process continued for half an hour, by which time the big map was beginning to look like the Milky Way. And suddenly Keybird called a halt.

'As many as we can reckon to raid simultaneously,' he said. 'We don't want these worthies to have much opportunity of ringing round to one another. A magistrate's been signing search warrants like mad all the time. Wonderful thing, English jurisprudence. My own fancy's for that one right down by the river. Useful derelict warehouse bang next door. So I'll wager – '

'No takers,' Honeybath said.

12

They were in a different car. Honeybath had glimpsed enough of it to judge it capable, on demand, of a wicked turn of speed. He had an alarmed vision of it as touching, later on during this unbelievable night, something quite phenomenal on the M4. But that would be all in the game. He was going to see this damned thing through. Even although he had to judge it not improbable that gentlemen who go about in pink Mercedes cars carry automatic weapons on their peregrinations as a matter of course.

Detective Superintendent Keybird's only weapon appeared to be a watch. With perhaps unnecessary drama, Honeybath thought of General Gordon, a light cane in his hand, confronting the Madhi's murderous horde in the Soudan. To remove his mind from this sort of thing, he endeavoured to engage Keybird in conversation.

'I've gathered,' he said, 'that this man Crumble is a known criminal. That was the reason of your being able to identify him from my sketch. But is bank robbery his particular line?'

'Oh, Crumble's a versatile villain.'

'I see.' It appeared to Honeybath that his simple question had produced an unexpected flicker or falter in the confidence which Keybird was now so determinedly radiating. This struck him as curious. 'At least in the main,' he persisted, 'you associate him with other forms of felony?'

'That's correct.' Keybird said this rather shortly. But then he seemed to recall that it was upon his own invitation that Honeybath was sitting in on the present operation. 'But not even naked felony, as often as not. You might call him a minor intriguer in what have tended to be pretty large-scale shady or borderline enterprises.'

'A negotiator? Sounding people out?'

'Very much that.'

'It was precisely his job with me, wouldn't you say?'

'Oh, very obviously. It was simply his assignment to dangle some carrot in front of you and lead you into a conveniently distant paddock.'

'That's very well put.' Honeybath didn't, in fact, feel that he had just been treated to one of Keybird's more felicitous speeches. 'But doesn't it suggest that, so far as this robbery goes, Crumble's role may have been as what they call a guest artist? Brought in to do his own characteristic turn, but not bound up with the main show in any close way?'

'He was there with your friends in the country.'

'Well, yes – but that, you may say, was to sustain in me the illusion that my commission made sense, if rather odd sense, in itself. And it removed him, just as it removed me, from the scene of the actual robbery. I suppose you hope to work from him, who is known to you, to the others, who are not. But you hardly expect, I take it, to find him actually sitting on the plunder?'

'We'll know quite soon now,' Keybird said. He had glanced at the watch. 'I expect you understand the conditions of the operation. Each of these possible hide-outs has to be effectively sealed off – and without causing alarm in a single one of them. No getaway by the back, or through an adjoining building, or over the roof. The chap there beside the driver' – Keybird pointed to the front of the car, where a dimly seen figure appeared to be carrying on a muttered colloquy with the ether at large – 'is checking off the dispositions one by one. About 200 officers involved, I'd say. When the last of them is in position I give the word to move in.'

'Most remarkable.' Honeybath was impressed, or at least felt he ought to be, by this military set-up. 'And we sit tight here as a kind of HQ?'

'Not exactly. We're just turning into Little Porges Street now, and the wharf is at the other end of it. In fact we're not more than a hundred yards from the river. The disused warehouse ought to be looming up somewhere on the left. Yes, there it is.' Keybird had been peering out into an East End gloom: a vista of what those not living in them are inclined to call mean streets – most of them feebly and crudely lit as if by some local council anxious to recapture the charms of the Victorian Age, a few of them for unknown reasons deluged in a brutal flood of raw electricity. The pubs had closed long ago, so there weren't many people about; their place had been taken, here and there by wisps and drifts of dun vapour from the Thames. From the Thames, too, came from time to time mournful nautical noises. Customs launches on the prowl for petty contraband, freighters just turned round and plodding sullenly off to the Antipodes once more, barges whose farthest ambition was the Isle of Dogs: only an expert ear could have discriminated their honks and wails and moanings.

'Stop and lights out,' Keybird said, with his habitual affectation of addressing empty air when giving orders. 'Midway between the next two lamp-posts.'

They glided to a halt in almost complete darkness. Nothing happened for what seemed a long time.

'Trouble in Hampstead,' the man in front reported unemotionally. 'They want another fifteen minutes, sir. Tricky stretch of roof-top in Upper Park Road.'

'OK. Fifteen minutes isn't worth a broken neck.' Keybird opened the door beside him. 'We'll stretch our legs.'

Honeybath recalled the last occasion upon which this proposition had been put to him. Out in the murk with his Detective Superintendent, he wondered whether he would presently turn round and find the police car to have vanished. But this was an uncontrolled and idle thought. Their four feet produced an alarming clump-clump in the deserted street. *With cat-like tread*, Honeybath thought to himself, and heard Sir Arthur Sullivan's tune faintly inside his head.

'HQ be damned,' Keybird said suddenly. The suggestion appeared to have irked him. 'I told you this place was my bet among the whole lot. And I go in first. It's the drill.'

'Crumble may be armed?'

'Lord, no! This isn't a gangster film.'

'Then can I come too?' It was with some surprise that Honeybath (eminent and elderly portrait painter) heard himself utter this small boy's plea.

'I'm afraid not. Definitely not. No danger – but too irregular by a long way. The Commissioner himself would hear of it and raise hell. Sorry. But you'll be all right outside.'

'I see,' Honeybath said, and this time heard obtrusive resignation in his own voice. But for his inner ear he murmured: 'And your Commissioner be damned too.'

It might have been said that the Honeybath blood was up.

Little Porges Street could readily have been taken for a cul-de-sac. It terminated in a high blank wall. But the last of the houses on its east side (which proved to be the house in which it was thought possible that Crumble lurked) incorporated in its structure a tunnel-like passage which gave upon a small wharf. On two sides of the wharf stood the abandoned warehouse, dimly distinguishable as a tall L-shaped building. On the fourth side flowed – or rather slopped and slapped – the river. The small, restless movement of the water round invisible timbers was the only sound to be heard.

'Contiguous,' Keybird murmured. 'It's probably quite possible to slip from one to the other. Interesting, wouldn't you say?'

Honeybath supposed it to be interesting – the fact, that is, that house and warehouse must own a considerable stretch of party-wall between them. He supposed, however, that what thieves would be most likely to secrete in a warehouse would be the millions of packets of cigarettes, or the hundreds of crates of whisky, which are constantly being hijacked from mammoth night-travelling lorries – although even more constantly, perhaps, on television than in real life. What you lifted from a bank, even on a large scale, could hardly require accommodation of this magnitude. But perhaps it was the simple getaway potential of the whole layout that Keybird judged to be promising.

Honeybath looked out over the river – itself invisible – and became aware that he was seeing something. His eyesight was good, and practised in fine accommodations. So he saw this dull dark shape seemingly floating in a void, and guessed at once that it was a police launch. The undistinguished dwelling at the end of Little Porges Street, and the warehouse which it adjoined, were really under siege. And so, it seemed, were almost a score of houses in and around London.

The darkness suddenly became alarming and horrible, and he looked up at the sky, as if there would be relief in a lavish, or even a meagre, show of stars. But, of course, there were no stars; there was only the dull angry glow – like the dome of Tophet stretching from horizon to horizon – which is London's lurid lid at night. Then he saw a light – a quick flash, instant and vanishing – on the roof of the warehouse. Once again, the police.

And, once again, the goggle-box world took hold of him. How many thrillers end up in an abandoned warehouse! The baddies are at bay, and armed. They race up staircases, preferably spiral ones. They shoot as they race. The emissaries of justice fire back, dodge behind vast and precariously balanced crates. The crates tumble; the cops fall deftly on their bellies behind bulging sacks, and continue to shoot. Some of them perform cunning outflanking manoeuvres, involving much personal hazard: they climb from window to window along exiguous ledges, or swing across yawning intervening spaces on conveniently dangling ropes. Some of the ropes end in enormous hooks, potent in hideous suggestiveness. The baddies have a concealed explosive device, conveniently disposed. The chief baddy's hand is on the plunger when a bullet gets him – probably bang between the eyes. He then – lest this should be judged inconclusive – disappears backwards through one of those upper apertures which, in warehouses, give so usefully upon nothing but a hundred-foot drop. Eventually –

Charles Honeybath realized that this was a foolish fantasy – and that he had been cautiously led back through the tunnel and into Little Porges Street. Keybird's hand was still on his elbow. And Keybird could just be distinguished as looking at his watch. And just distinguishable, too, was an unimpressive and ancient van drawn up by the kerb. It might have represented the last hope of an indigent itinerant greengrocer. A torch momentarily flickered, and Honeybath saw that the van was loaded not with potatoes but with policemen. Such a huddle of helmeted men couldn't look other than absurd, and the whole deployment of manpower seemed altogether excessive for the rounding up of the insignificant rascal he remembered as Peach – or even for the rounding up, as it were, of a whole basket of Peaches. One had to assume that Peach's or Crumble's conjectured associates were altogether more desperate characters. Presumably the larger the robbery the heavier the penalty if you were caught. (Honeybath found himself – fatefully, as it was to turn out – wondering about the ethics of this.) And these people had achieved an enormous haul. They had to be thought of as playing for high stakes, either way. If there were by chance a number of them inside this dark and silent house, it was possible that one had to be prepared for their trying to shoot their way out.

But it was precisely the complete absence of any sign of such preparation that struck Honeybath in the next ten minutes. The policemen had debouched from the van, and gave the effect of filling the narrow street. There was another batch on the wharf, and there were certainly several on the roof. A couple of Radar-like dogs were also in evidence. But the equipment of this assault force appeared to consist entirely of electric torches and walkie-talkies. Perhaps the constables concealed, presumably down a trouser-leg, truncheons not much modified since the age of Dogberry and Verges. But of fire-arms there wasn't a sign. An odd tradition, Honeybath thought. And he suddenly felt rather proud of mucking in with Keybird and his crowd, even if as a mere indulged spectator.

The house was no longer in complete darkness. A dim and respectable light had appeared behind a curtained upper window;

what it somehow suggested to Honeybath was the aged widow of some blameless petty shopkeeper in the district betaking herself to bed. Probably this whole foray would prove a farce, and Crumble turn out to be anywhere but in this particular hypothetical retreat.

Keybird was on the doorstep, flanked by two constables – and with one of these was one of the dogs. A position on the pavement had been indicated to Honeybath; and he supposed that from its security he was to continue his passive participation in the affair. Keybird looked at his watch for the last time, raised a hand, and knocked on the door. It was a loud knock, but there was nothing dramatic about it. And, having knocked, he patiently waited. The place was a sealed box, after all. Nothing happened.

Keybird knocked again. This time, and presumably as a consequence, the light in the upper room went out. Whereupon Keybird spoke – again undramatically, and with what might have been termed only a token or ritual loudness.

'We are police officers,' Keybird said. 'Open the door.' In the same instant that he produced his injunction the two constables hurled themselves forward with staggering momentum. The door gave way before them with a splintering crash. Honeybath felt that he was at least learning all the time.

Keybird, the two mobile battering-rams, the deutero-Radar: these all disappeared together into a darkness rendered only the more confusing by a sort of maniacal torchlight ballet. Honeybath, watching his chance on the pavement, saw that there was in fact no choice before him. A solid mass of policemen was now hurtling forward; he was caught up in it regardlessly and swept along like a bathing child overtaken by a wave and tumbled on the beach.

One resents being jostled. But this jostling had inadvertently got Honeybath precisely where he wanted to be: in on the final act of an undeniably exciting drama. It was therefore illogical of him to feel resentful. But the surging policemen had been so big and so young and so little inclined to notice him that he did find himself nourishing the emotion, midway between irritation and anger, which it has more than once been necessary to record him as subject to. It didn't last long. But it lasted long enough to produce what was certainly the most startlingly aberrant piece of conduct his entire course of life had produced as far. (Others lay ahead.)

There was a narrow little hall, with a narrow little staircase running straight up one side of it. There were doors to right and left, and ahead there was a glass door, displeasingly coloured, which must lead to such domestic offices as a miserable dwelling of this order might boast of. So much Honeybath could distinguish by torchlight – as also the fact that the whole area afforded singularly little space for manoeuvre. Several policemen had plunged at a rapid lumber into the room on the left; it was observable that they all wore stiff and cumbersome greatcoats which gave their movements an impeded and robot-like air. Moments later they lumbered out again; and it was now that one of them, a sergeant, for the first time remarked Honeybath's unauthorized though not exactly voluntary presence. He stared in horror.

'In here,' the sergeant said peremptorily. 'And don't stir again until you're told to.' And he actually took Honeybath (schoolfellow of the Prime Minister and First Lord of the Treasury) by the shoulders and propelled him into the room. He then banged the door shut on him, and left him to his own devices.

When the injured artist had recovered breath it took him only a second to see why it was only for seconds that the apartment had detained the constabulary. It was small, unfurnished, and untenanted. There was a damp, musty smell. A hideous and discoloured paper depended in strips from the walls. Somebody, apparently moved by a spasm of decent aesthetic feeling, must have torn down several residual strips of it, for there was a small heap of the stuff on the middle of the floor. All this was clearly visible, since the departing sergeant had been thoughtful enough to flick a switch which turned on a single naked light in the centre of the ceiling.

There must be a breeze coming from somewhere, because the wallpaper on the floor was stirring gently. Having nothing better to do, Honeybath went over to the single window and endeavoured to peer out. There was little to be seen, however, and he turned back into the room. Where the wallpaper had been he now viewed a black rectangular hole. And Crumble (or Peach) was standing beside this improbable theatrical trapdoor with a revolver in his hand.

'So it's you,' Crumble said (or, rather, snarled – which is proper on such occasions). He pointed the weapon straight at Honeybath's chest. 'Get out of my way!'

'Don't be silly, Mr Crumble.' Honeybath – the subliminal Honeybath whom we have so regularly to reckon with – said this quite calmly. 'You may kill or maim me, no doubt. You may do the same by five of these policemen. And then you'll be finished, since there will be a dozen left to get on top of you. Fairly literally, I suspect. And you'll still not be looking too good when you arrive in the dock. It's behaviour they don't at all like.'

Crumble – or the wretched little Peach, who had so laboriously got to Lesson Six – stared stupidly at Honeybath. Then he stared, equally stupidly, at the weapon now trembling dangerously in his own hand.

'It's another five years,' he said hoarsely. 'A distinct charge, and the sentences to run consecutive. Possessing and threatening to use a bloody gun.'

'You might have thought of that. And it's no good' – Honeybath had detected incipient movement on Crumble's part – 'thinking to chuck the thing through that window. There are plenty of them out there too.' There was a moment's silence. Crumble looked very like Peach – the Peach whom Honeybath had sketched so triumphantly. And an artist is in a very special relationship to anybody or anything that he has thus made his own. Honeybath was in no such relationship with all those charging policemen. 'Give it to me,' he said suddenly. And he walked up to Crumble, took the revolver from his unresisting hand, and dropped it into his own coat-pocket. Then he moved to the door, opened it, and called out.

'Sergeant, Mr Crumble is here with me in this room.'

PART THREE

HONEYBATH INVESTIGATES

13

The police had handcuffed Crumble. It ought to have appeared – at least to Honeybath's private knowledge – a reasonable precaution: the man, after all, had been lethally brandishing a revolver only a few minutes before. But the police were unaware of this; and Detective Superintendent Keybird, indeed, had brusquely pooh-poohed the notion that Crumble could conceivably be armed.

In any case, Honeybath found he didn't like the sight of those ugly metal manacles on Crumble (formerly Peach). There was a dreadful indignity about the thing which the mere fact of the man's being a crook didn't somehow palliate in the slightest degree. Then there was the point that it was Honeybath himself who had really caught Crumble. He had done all those dicks' job for them, perhaps been instrumental in returning several of them other than as corpses to their wives and kiddies, and generally deserved the Queen's Commendation for Bravery, or whatever it was called. But in all this he found he took no satisfaction at all. He seemed to be quite without the sense of virtue in which any rational citizen would surely, in his situation, be entitled to bask. And he increasingly hated having made that sketch of Peach. It would be exhibited in court when the chap was put on trial, he supposed, and eventually filed away at Scotland Yard in some kind of Rogues' Gallery.

Then there was the fact that Keybird appeared in not too good a humour. That Crumble, and Crumble alone, had been found in this nasty little house was plainly contrary to his expectations. It was equally clear that the prospect of a magistrate, and then a judge and jury, having to be told of Mr Charles Honeybath's role in the arrest didn't please him at all; his underlying feeling was evidently that Honeybath had barged in where he had no business to be, and had embarrassingly complicated what would have been an entirely simple affair. Honeybath, thinking of that revolver (which was still in his pocket), saw the matter somewhat differently, but was unable to say so. All this ended up in his saying, rather abruptly, that he would be obliged if he might now be driven back to his flat. There was a great hunt still going on. But whether or not they found all that stolen money was something about which he found he couldn't care less.

As first the East End of London and then the Embankment slid past, he wondered whether he could possibly sleep a wink after such a staggering day. But, as it turned out, a blessed oblivion overcame him in the moment that his head touched the pillow. He had a flair for sleep.

He was boiling himself an egg – a shade late in the morning, it was true – when there was a knock on his front door. Since the door was provided with an electric bell in respectable working order, this mode of summons was unnecessary. But even as he reflected on this, Honeybath reflected, too, that it was a familiar knock. He had heard it not long ago. In other words, Keybird was on top of him again. It struck him with sudden force that he hadn't got clear of the affair simply by requiring to be sent home on the previous night. In whatever criminal proceeding emerged from it he would himself inevitably be a key witness. It was an alarming thought. Moreover what he ought to be turning to at once was the business of fixing up those two new commissions. Further colloquy with the police – unless it was directly in the interest of recovering that portrait – was the last thing he wanted to give time to. So it was in some displeasure that he went to the door and opened it.

Keybird shook hands with him – an expansive gesture which proved to be the issue of a buoyant mood. The man was disgustingly jubilant. But at least it wasn't simply because he had the wretched

Crumble locked up. It was because the proceeds of the bank robbery had been recovered *in toto.*

Honeybath received the news with civil expressions of gratification, but inwardly confronted the fact that he didn't care a damn. He much doubted whether (apart from Keybird and Co., who were going to get the kudos) anybody stood much to benefit by this triumph of the law. He was certainly fairly sure that nobody would have been the worse had no penny ever turned up again. It must be the bank's business not to let your money or securities be carried off by thieves; the bank would have had to pay up to everybody – with profuse apologies into the bargain; and the actual liability would have spread out and out, like diminishing ripples on the surface of a pool, until it vanished as anything distinguishable at all on the farther verges of the most distant insurance corporations. It wouldn't have been a bit like the loss of a unique work of art. Of a portrait, for instance.

The stuff had been found in the warehouse, all neatly packed in securely sealed biscuit-tins. It could have been trundled utterly inviolate from one end of England to the other that way. So it was no doubt fortunate that the police had made it as expeditiously as they had. They had to thank their computer for that – and Honeybath's portrait sketch.

'And what about the rest of the gang?' Honeybath asked with engaging eagerness. It had come to him that here was what Keybird might have called his Achilles heel. 'Are they all rounded up?'

'Well, no. In fact none of them are. But it's only a matter of time. We can lean on Crumble a bit, for a start.'

'Lean on him?' The term was unfamiliar to Honeybath.

'Crumble may cough.'

'Cough? Has the poor fellow caught a cold? He isn't tubercular?' Honeybath sounded anxious. 'He doesn't strike me as having a very robust constitution.'

'To hell with his constitution.' Keybird was looking at Honeybath with the most pronounced policemanly suspicion. 'And you know perfectly well what I mean. The man's small fry, I admit. But he remains our only certain link with the thing.'

'What about Arbuthnot and Mr X – and Sister Agnes, for that matter?' Here was Honeybath's principal point of irritation emerging again. 'Isn't it about time to go for them bald-headed?'

'Oh, they'll be caught up with sooner or later. But they probably aren't exactly the big fish either.'

'They hang out in a big way.'

'That's true.' Keybird had one of his rare checks. 'But I doubt whether the main line goes back to them.'

The main line, Honeybath thought. Of what used to be the Great Western Railway. He made to speak – and then he too checked himself. He temporized.

'I don't follow you,' he said. 'And I still think you ought to follow *them*. What do you mean – not the main line?'

'They may have a showy set-up. But they were acting as no more than a temporary dumping-ground, weren't they?'

'A dumping-ground?'

'For yourself, sir. Just a minor job, you might say, contracted out to them. They mayn't have known what was really going on.'

'But Crumble – '

'There are obscurities, of course. We mustn't expect to get the entire picture clear at once.'

'They paid me all that money – and half of it without – '

'It's a bit of a puzzle, I agree. But first things first.'

Honeybath had heard this expression before. The mingled acuteness and obtuseness of this high-ranking sleuth was now infuriating him. And this made it the more tiresome that he no longer had a clear conscience in regard to the man. There was that confounded revolver. It was locked up – loaded, he had observed, in all six chambers – within a few feet of where he and Keybird were sitting. Not that he regretted what he had done. It had been a simple compassionate action, and there had been nothing in him that could have avoided it. He knew that it is crimes against property which are most heavily punished by the law, and that Crumble was booked for a long stretch in any case. To get him off an additional whack had been merely humane and sensible.

'Mr Keybird,' he asked coldly, ' – is there anything more that I can do for you? I have several pressing professional engagements in front of me.' He almost stood up, but decided this would be uncivil. 'And I suppose my studio can now be returned to me?'

'Oh, certainly.' Keybird paused. 'And you mustn't think we're neglecting your odd experience.' In Honeybath's now heated imagination Keybird's manner of saying this was insufferably indulgent and whimsical. 'We must certainly get those people. And you could, you know, perform another great service for us. You could sketch them too.'

Honeybath might have expected this, and it was surprising that the suggestion took him aback as it did. Here, after all, was the line of immediate inquiry that he was pressing for. And of course he could sketch the villainous Arbuthnot and the unfortunate Mr X. Sister Agnes and the chauffeur and both the menservants too, for that matter. And he would have to do it. He couldn't decently decline. He didn't even know why he had a lurking impulse to decline. He was chiefly aware that he wanted his breakfast, that the coffee would have gone cold, and that he'd have to start in on boiling another egg. What was really stirring in his mind – and it was quite something – stirred for the moment only at a level below that of cogitation.

But when Keybird went away, having received a decent assurance that the sketches would be made, Honeybath drank a cup of tepid coffee quite without thinking, forgot about his egg entirely, and gave himself up to a moody perambulation of his sitting-room. He paused once to unlock the drawer in which he had deposited Crumble's weapon, but refrained from handling the thing when it was once more under his regard. He had a muzzy sense that he mustn't leave his fingerprints on it, or obliterate Crumble's fingerprints, although this was obviously a rubbishing notion out of cheap fiction. What was true was that he had come into possession of an extremely sinister object, the uses of which were in a world of which he knew nothing at all. He would leave it where it was until nightfall, and then walk to the Embankment and drop it into the river. In the ooze of Thames as it flowed beneath London's bridges must lie innumerable weapons which, through the centuries, it had been convenient for their owners to part with unobtrusively. And most of those people would have been guilty of some crime.

Honeybath suddenly saw himself performing this clandestine act. He heard the splash. And he had attracted the attention of a policeman – a policeman who had appeared from nowhere and who must actually have been standing beside him as the revolver fell to the water. He recalled that giving this twist to private fantasy was one of the most annoying tricks of his mind; he couldn't imagine some mildly culpable course of conduct without its finishing up in a vivid mental image of ingeniously brought-about exposure and disgrace. He locked up the gun again – and as he did so had an even stranger vision of himself as handcuffed to it, much as poor Crumble had been handcuffed to himself.

Determinedly he sat down to the telephone, with the laudable intention of sorting out his bread and butter over the next couple of months. It turned out that the retiring headmaster was preparing for the strains and stresses of approaching idleness by taking a short holiday in Crete, and that the Master of the Higglers and Tranters was only beginning to recover from a severe attack of mumps. The commissions were secure, but Honeybath had time on his hands.

It ought to have been a satisfactory discovery; he had, after all, quite something to recover from himself. He almost rang up BEA or Olympic Airways to inquire about the next flight to Rhodes. Almost unaccountably to himself, he rang up British Rail instead. And it was the departure-time of trains to Swansea that he found himself jotting down.

14

The next thing was a map, and the next thing after that again was quite a lot of maps. First, that was to say, he must treat himself to a bird's eye view of the entire south of England, and then he must think of himself as to be equipped for a pretty long walking-tour from London towards Swansea. Not that he intended actually to walk. That would take much too long – in addition to which plodding along a permanent way was probably illegal and would certainly be uncomfortable. He must simply travel by train – again and again, if necessary – while keeping his eyes open. He decided that Ordnance Survey maps on the scale of 1:25,000 would be the thing. That was about $2^{1}/_{2}$ inches to one mile. He'd need the devil of a lot of them, and on a fast train he'd have to fish out a fresh one about every five minutes. Moreover his behaviour might seen distinctly odd to any fellow passengers. But at least he'd always know exactly what he was looking at through the window.

Equipping himself in this and certain other ways turned out to afford Charles Honeybath considerable pleasure. Years dropped away from him. He was no longer Honeybath RA. He was once more Honeybath Minor (Honeybath Major had been his elder brother, now with God) and his main ambition in life was one day to become a King's Scout. He had already obtained, he recalled, his Pathfinder's Badge. Which was a good start. He had also done rather well in what, during his public-school days, had still been called the OTC. Hadn't he, in fact, gained his Cert. A? Certainly he had gained his Cert. A. Impressive field officers who had journeyed from the War Office to conduct the examination had specially commended the masterly manoeuvre by which he had outflanked and captured a massively defended Junior Changing Shed. And of course there had been a great deal of map-reading involved as well. He was quite certain he remembered his remarkable performance at that. If he *had* had a war (and the fact that he hadn't might have been pointed to by a psychologist as the reason for his being particularly pleased that he was carrying a purloined and fully loaded revolver in his pocket now) – if he *had* had a war there could be little doubt that he would have ended up unerringly piloting whole divisions to their goal across the almost featureless wastes of North Africa.

He had been dumped out of that damned car – he now knew – not all that distance from Basingstoke, an uninteresting place associated in his mind only with some foolish joke in a comic opera. But Basingstoke was neither here nor there, since it might be separated from Mr X's residence (or Mr Basil Arbuthnot's lair or den) by sixty miles or more. Indeed, that problematical dwelling might lie as far west along the railway as, say, Chipping Sodbury. And what about the other direction? He was almost certain that what he was looking for would not be found east of Didcot, let alone east of Goring or Reading. His Oxford days (and singularly useless they had been) had been largely given over to hurrying up to London to haunt the studios of real live artists and to batter on the doors of the Slade. As it had taken him two years to achieve the entrée there he had come to know the Oxford – Didcot – Paddington stretch uncommonly well. And Castle Arbuthnot just didn't have the feel of that terrain.

But from Didcot to Chipping Sodbury wasn't a mere step. It would probably be physically or nervously impossible to keep up a furlong-by-furlong vigilance. He would almost certainly have to have several goes at it. It looked as if British Rail was going to lift quite a lot of money off him. He was so resigned to this that he even briefly considered the advantage of buying some sort of season ticket.

As it turned out, that would have been a mistake.

He thought at first that he was going to have a first-class compartment to himself. This would be enormously advantageous. He could spread out his maps as he pleased, and nobody passing up or down the corridor would be likely much to notice the fact. But of course somebody might push in on him further down the line. Perhaps he ought to have reserved the whole compartment. The First Lord of the Treasury (former schoolfellow of Honeybath Minor) certainly travelled like that – although no doubt with a bodyguard lurking near at hand. Or even simple dukes or marquises, repairing to the seclusion of a country seat. But a private citizen – Honeybath reflected – might only attract undesirable curiosity by so lavish a proceeding. Besides which, the cost would make quite a hole in that still-to-be-earned £2,520.

At the last moment chance provided him with a fellow-passenger, after all. Almost as the train moved out of the station, a young woman tumbled in on him. A very pretty girl, he told himself – and was then surprised at his own momentary impercipience. She wasn't a very pretty girl; she was that vastly different and much rarer thing, a very beautiful one. In his professional character, he knew perfectly well that it is pointless, or at least hazardous, to declare one woman more beautiful than another: the mysterious attribute can vanish even as you pause to admire; can declare itself suddenly in what you would think to pass by unregardingly. Still, this girl was beautiful. It even occurred to him that she might prove undesirably distracting later on. But until Didcot, at least, he could glance discreetly at her now and then. In fact, he presently discovered, he could sit and stare at her if he wanted to. For she was not the sort of girl who sits idly in a railway carriage, dividing her time between turning over the pages of a rubbishing magazine and glancing – or staring – at you. She was of a studious habit; and, indeed, you quickly saw that her beauty itself was of a somewhat severe and intellectual order. Her travelling impedimenta consisted of two books: a big one and a little one. She had put the big one down on the seat beside her; it had a sombre cover on which was pasted the label of the London Library. The little one was a paperback of the egghead sort, and Honeybath saw that it was called *Keynes and After*. This the young woman had opened near the middle and became absorbed in. So Honeybath was able to observe her. He observed that her skirt came almost to her knees and that her shoes were of a conjoined plainness and elegance not readily to be come by very far from Rome or Milan. (He had to be something of an expert in such matters: feet, like hands, are expensive extras.) Honeybath saw that he was probably in the company of the daughter of a duke, making off for the weekend to the parental home, but only on the basis of having so far broken free of its influence as to pursue rigorous if sadly plebeian studies at the London School of Economics.

These reflections, together with a little more or less covert fiddling with his maps, took our investigator through a pause at Reading and on to Didcot. Throughout this period the girl didn't look up from her treatise except to check the names of these railway stations. At Reading, indeed, she did accompany this exercise with a glance at Honeybath. It was an impersonal and almost unflatteringly uninterested glance. She might have been checking on him too, and deciding that he was the sort of little man who came to wind the clocks or tune the pianos or carry out minor dental operations without any impertinent suggestion that these might be more readily achieved in his surgery – or in his dental parlour, as the girl's father would doubtless phrase it.

Honeybath had just arrived at this assessment of himself in the supposed regard of the young woman sitting diagonally to him in the compartment – had arrived at it, naturally, without gratification, even if with no particular resentment – when the young woman looked up once more and gave him a brilliant smile. It wasn't a smile that seemed occasioned by anything in particular, and it somehow carried the suggestion of being definitely not intended as a prelude to even the most casual conversation. It was almost as if she had realized that her first glance might have occasioned misapprehension and she was now anxious to make a brief amends. If the smile *had* been motivated in any way it had been by that. Honeybath preferred to think that it had been an entirely spontaneous – as it was certainly a merely momentary – thing. He felt as if he had been glancingly well-regarded by a passing goddess.

But now he had to apply himself in earnest to his task. The Swansea train, having turned away disdainfully from the line to Oxford and other obscure cathedral cities, was heading for the estuary of the Severn and the Principality of Wales. The Vale of the White Horse and much more or less open country lay immediately ahead, and most of the railway-stations (being small and helpless ones) had been closed through the zeal of the celebrated Lord Beeching. Wantage Road, Challow Station, Uffington Junction: little, if anything, would prove to be going forward in these former busy haunts of men. And haunts of racehorses, Honeybath recalled, since it was a region given over rather to quadrupedal than to bipedal forms of life. But this uncrowded character made the region, for him, a promising one. He got out his first map.

The proceeding left the young woman incurious. In fact it now became possible to believe that the young woman was rather sleepy; she had closed her succinct exposition of recent economic theory, and was now closing her eyes as well. This wasn't entirely a gain. It did mean that Honeybath wouldn't be embarrassed by the consciousness of being observed as indulging in eccentric behaviour. On the other hand it made an absorbed contemplation of beauty into a possibility entirely devoid of offence. So long as the young woman slept he could goggle at her as he pleased. Moreover there is something peculiarly seductive about a sleeping girl. The spectacle releases fancies not conducive to edification. Honeybath realized that he must keep his eye resolutely on the ball.

The ball was whatever dwellings of the more imposing sort presented themselves at only a moderate remove on the left as the train hurtled west. Honeybath quickly came to realize that there weren't going to be many of them. When the Great Western Railway had first been laid down it had been taken for granted that the line wouldn't venture into the near vicinity of the territorial nobility or the landed gentry. Later on, people with the money and ambition to build themselves big new houses had naturally kept away from it.

More often than not, the really grand places had the Thames between themselves and this all but modern means of vulgar locomotion.

And what exactly was he looking for, anyway? A private park of modest proportions, fairly densely wooded on its northern boundary, but with a gap in the trees through which it ought to be possible to view a mansion the dimensions and exterior appearance of which were almost totally unknown to him. It should be no farther away than would enable a man to decipher, through good binoculars, a small placard exhibited, say, in one of its windows. And before this scene it seemed that, just occasionally, an express train such as this made a brief and grudging pause.

Was he to expect any signs of life? It had been ventured by Detective Superintendent Keybird, in one of his pooh-poohing moods, that the mysterious domicile of Mr X would by now be an empty shell. The whole show had merely been briefly mounted, that was to say, to take Honeybath in. Most of the house would have been empty and untenanted all the time. Just a few rooms would have been rigged up for occupation. Honeybath had vaguely heard of film companies doing something like this: taking over, briefly and on the cheap, some useless and abandoned mansion with the object of using such bits and pieces of it as they required.

Suddenly (and as he briskly substituted one large-scale map for another) he became aware of a circumstance that seemed decidedly to support this hypothesis. He hadn't thought of it before. Peach-Crumble had been part of the *entourage* to be met with *chez* Arbuthnot. But in almost no time after Honeybath's own departure from the place Peach-Crumble had been reduced to cowering in a miserable dockside dwelling in the East End of London. That did rather suggest, so to speak, a folding of tents like the Arabs, silently stealing away.

Yet this was really no argument at all. The booty from the bank had been hidden in London. Crumble, as a responsible member of the gang, had simply been despatched to look after it as soon as he no longer had a role as one of Mr X's attendants or warders. Then again, there had been all those cars, and all those men – after some quite noisy conference – piling into them and driving away. Unless Honeybath had positively dreamed up all that, it blankly contradicted the proposition that the entire charade had been mounted, in the most ephemeral way, for his, Honeybath's, sole benefit.

And here he was on the verge of a much larger consideration. It might be called, without pretentiousness, his own deepest intuition about the whole affair. Or not exactly an intuition, since it was something for which there existed a thoroughly intellectual basis. What in general is called proportion had been one of the main studies of Honeybath's life. And the Keybird vision of the thing violated his sense of proportion. As a mere means of securing, for the space of a fortnight, the absence from his studio of an artist of the most modest fame, the imposture in which he had been involved was just too elaborate by half. Contemplate it fairly and squarely, and it simply didn't stand up. The bank robbery had been only a venture, after all. It might have been wrecked, well or merely immediately before its successful accomplishment, by any sort of mischance or miscalculation. Yet very large sums of money (not even counting that second dollop of his fee) would have had to be staked on it, and it alone, if Keybird's theory were the valid one. Reflect on this, and you came upon a very surprising conclusion indeed. The Arbuthnot set-up was not an ephemeral, an *ad hoc* affair. It subserved other and larger ends than the single *coup* which had met disaster at the efficient hands of Detective Superintendent Keybird and his 200 constables. What Honeybath RA was himself now hunting down could be nothing but the permanent headquarters of some vast criminal organization.

Rather unexpectedly, and in the middle of nowhere, the train had come to a halt.

15

It was like a dream – a through-the-looking-glass dream. Everything was there, but everything was the wrong way round. There was the train, but he was looking *from* the train. There was the house, but he was looking *at* the house. There was the gap in the trees, hut it was quite close up on him instead of quite far away. And the house was *just* a house, precisely as the train had been *just* a train until he got those binoculars on it. A large house, but totally anonymous. It rang no bell with him. But then there was no reason why it should. He had never once been able to stand back from it and view it *coup d'oeil* before.

All this – if only in the suddenness of its appearing – was disconcerting and confusing. Honeybath sat goggling through the window, with his litter of abruptly needless maps around him. And then the train – which, after the habit of pausing trains, had not quite lost momentum after all – the train gave itself an indignant twitch, and within seconds had achieved an accelerated motion in the direction of the now westering sun.

The scene had rung no bell, Honeybath repeated to himself, and was conscious of the phrase as carrying some obscure ambiguity. The scene had vanished – and now, in no time, its entire rural context would for a while vanish too. What lay ahead must be the shocking city of Swindon – full, no doubt, of enjoying and suffering human beings much like himself, but decidedly without marked aesthetic appeal. He would get out of the train there, possibly hire a car, and then –

And then *what*? He had really made no plan; hadn't thought beyond just locating the enemy on the map. And he hadn't even done this – although it would be only a moment's work now. He knew to within half a mile the position at which the train had paused seconds ago. His finger was still on the spot. And there – precisely at the tip of a well-tended nail – was the conventional representation of a small piece of parkland, and in the middle of it a black rectangle and the words *Imlac House*. An odd name, but that was it. Imlac House. He peered backwards through his window, on the off-chance that a glimpse of this residence might still be offering. But, naturally enough, it had vanished from view. It must now be at least a mile away.

And the girl was looking at him curiously.

'Excuse me,' the girl said. 'Are you making some sort of survey of English country houses?' She spoke rather as if she expected Honeybath would reveal himself as having an American accent, but at the same time with a polite confidence which somehow made her barging in like this quite inoffensive. Honeybath had an impulse to agree that he was doing just that. It wouldn't be a bad cover for the eccentric show he had been putting up. And it looked as if the young woman hadn't been so sound asleep as he had supposed.

'Well, no,' Honeybath said (thinking better of this). 'But I am quite interested in the place we have just passed. It's called Imlac House.' The girl, it occurred to him, might well live in the district, and have some useful information to give. 'Do you happen to know anything about it?'

'Well, yes – I think I can say I do.' The girl was looking at him oddly. 'Just why are you taking an interest in it?'

'I was there quite recently – professionally, and for nearly a fortnight. I happen – '

'That hardly explains why you should be concerned to spot it from a train with the aid of a map.' The young woman had produced this challenge crisply. It was to be feared that she was rapidly coming to

119

view Honeybath as a highly suspicious character. 'Did you take a great fancy to it?'

'Nothing of the kind. In fact, I can hardly be said to have seen it at all.'

'In a fortnight!'

'It certainly sounds odd. But the circumstances were unusual. I arrived in the dark, and came away in the dark too. And all I saw of the house was the rooms I lived and worked in. That, and a walled garden. Oh, and a lift. By the way, may I say my name is Charles Honeybath? I'm a portrait-painter.' Honeybath rather hoped that the girl might be familiar with his name, and find it reassuring. But this didn't happen. On the contrary, the girl's glance was now positively hostile.

'And my name is Diana Mariner,' she said. 'Mr Honeybath, is this some sort of stupid joke?'

'Nothing of the kind.' Honeybath was indignant. 'Why should you suppose anything of the sort?'

'Simply because I live at Imlac House. I'm going home there now.'

'How very interesting!' If Honeybath had been dumbfounded he supposed he had successfully dissimulated the fact. Could this upper-class female economist in whom he had so rashly begun to confide be a daughter of the unspeakable Arbuthnot, and perhaps wholly ignorant of her father's evil ways? A crucial question occurred to him. 'May I ask, Miss Mariner, whether you have been away from home for long?'

'For two years, as a matter of fact. From *this* home, that is – the one you seem to have been staying in some rather odd way. We have a smaller house somewhere else. Daddy lets Imlac when he has to go away for long periods. He's an ambassador, you see – although really he's an admiral.'

'An admiral?'

'Admiral Mariner. So you can tell – can't you? – that he's only a sort of amateur diplomat. Not what they call a career one. And about Imlac – well, he only got possession again a couple of days ago. I expect the place is in an awful mess. Not that the man who rented it didn't have all the right references. And we only use one wing when we're there ourselves. I suppose it's because Daddy hasn't got very much money. Anyway, I'm longing to get back. I love Imlac, and wish he didn't have to turn an honest penny that way.'

'Most understandable.' Honeybath was probably staring stupidly at Miss Mariner. She was no longer hostile; indeed, it must be said that she had turned surprisingly, if ramblingly, communicative. And that such invaluable information as this (which he dimly began to see as fitting into the entire mystery plausibly enough) should tumble by sheer coincidence into his lap was a gift of fortune such as he could scarcely have hoped for.

'But I still find something rather odd in what you've told me, Mr Honeybath. About hardly moving freely around Imlac at all. Were the people very eccentric or something?'

'Decidedly so. Or at least it may be expressed that way.'

'I just can't understand it.' The largeness of Miss Mariner's astonishment before the not very striking facts which had been communicated to her might have struck Detective Superintendent Keybird (had he been present) as almost obtrusive. 'And do you mean you were there to paint a portrait?'

'Certainly I was.'

'You were painting Colonel Bunbury himself?'

'Colonel Bunbury?' Honeybath was aware that he was feeling slightly giddy.

'That's the name of our tenant at Imlac – the one who has just quit.'

'No, I wasn't painting anybody with that name. I was painting –' Honeybath broke off. If he announced that he had been painting somebody called Mr X it was probable that Miss Mariner would conclude him to be mad (he was rather wondering about this himself) and make a dive for the communication cord. 'Imlac seemed to be in the possession of a man called Arbuthnot – Basil Arbuthnot.'

'I don't understand it at all.' Diana Mariner was looking perplexed, but fortunately not alarmed. 'It seems to me that something uncommonly funny has been going on. I'm not sure that my father hasn't been wondering a little, as a matter of fact.'

'It's a pity that he hasn't wondered to better effect.' Honeybath judged it fair enough to offer this astringent remark. 'Something very funny indeed has been going on.' He looked steadily at Admiral Mariner's learned daughter – so recently no more than a young stranger with an interest in economic theory. 'And connected with a very big bank robbery, I think I ought to say. Brutally put, Miss Mariner, your father has been renting Imlac to a bunch of crooks.'

There was a moment's silence. Honeybath wondered whether he had done very wrong in thus so abruptly introducing an innocent child to the horrors of criminal life. The train rattled through a station which he vaguely supposed to be Shrivenham. They would be in Swindon in a very few minutes.

'I don't see why a bunch of crooks should want you to paint a portrait.'

'No more do I.' Honeybath was impressed by the immediate clarity of Miss Mariner's observation. It came, he supposed, of a severe academic training. 'It's what I'm trying to find out. And I want to get back my portrait. That's why I'm on this confounded train.'

'You mean you're coming to visit us?'

'Well, not exactly. Obviously not, in a way, since I haven't been aware of your existence.'

'I think you'd better, all the same.' Miss Mariner said this decisively and almost threateningly. 'You owe my father an explanation, it seems to me.'

'A good many people are owed explanations.'

'Including the police, I'd think. Are you just doing this on your own, Mr Honeybath?'

'Well, yes – so far as this particular move goes.' The girl had again been unnervingly quick on the ball. 'The police don't seem to be quite so interested in my portrait as I am. So – '

'That's natural, I'd say, if they have a big robbery on their plate. But will you come and see my father – now? Just to explain things a little.'

'Yes, of course – if you want me to.' It didn't appear possible to give Diana Mariner any other reply than this. 'But if you think, in the light of what I've told you, that you should go first to the local police – '

'I shouldn't think local police would be much good in an affair like this.'

'You're probably right.' Honeybath had his own unfortunate encounter with a rural constabulary still freshly in mind. 'How do we get to your house?'

'They'll have left my Mini in the station car park. It's our usual arrangement. And here we are.'

There were two car parks, it seemed, and Miss Mariner's modest conveyance might be in either. She went off to hunt for it, leaving Honeybath with a brisk injunction to stay put. So he stood in the big station yard and waited – much occupied with his own reflections, and not greatly attending to what went on around him. He had a strong but confused sense that just these few minutes were affording him a useful chance of working out the implications of his abruptly transformed situation. His quarry had fled and only their late domicile remained – a domicile now returned to its just proprietor, a respect able and indeed no doubt eminent public servant, to whom he, Honeybath, was going to have an uncommonly unlikely-sounding story to tell. But what was *not* unlikely-sounding in this whole affair? And even when anything *did* sound likely ought he to think of accepting it without a good deal of caution? For instance –

Honeybath found that something which had been hovering in his head was eluding him, and that what he was chiefly conscious of was a slight chill in the air. He was standing in shade, and the station yard was being visited by an unfriendly breeze. But there was sunshine only a few yards away, and a high brick wall which probably caught and radiated an agreeable warmth. He strolled over to it. The girl – Miss Mariner, Diana Mariner – was taking rather a long time to find her car. He wondered whether it was refusing to start, or had been pinned in by some unscrupulous fellow-motorist. The station yard itself was fairly busy, but so large that the traffic seemed able to charge around in rather a carefree way. Directly in front of Honeybath now, a heavy lorry had begun to back with surprising speed out of a bonnet-to-pavement row of similar vehicles. He speculated, quite idly, on whether it would wheel to left or right. He saw that it was doing neither, but simply continuing to back – and at a speed which could only be judged not so much dangerous as completely mad. Unless –

Honeybath found that he had achieved a miraculous sideways jump, and had done so in the split-second of realizing that sudden death was hurtling at him. But the jump didn't get him clear by any means. He was conscious of a terrific force catching him he didn't know where. Tumbled to the ground, he was aware for a moment only of similarly tumbling bricks. Then he saw a gaping hole in the wall against which he had been standing. The tail of the lorry was in some way jammed in it. The lorry was screaming in rage or agony – presumably because it was frantically trying to extricate itself and get away. The lorry suddenly clanked and clattered instead of screaming, and then fell silent. The driver jumped from the cab, and for a moment stood halted and irresolute. He was dressed – Honeybath's senses were at once acute and chaotic – as the drivers of such vehicles commonly are dressed. But, in fact, he was Mr Basil Arbuthnot's (or was it Mr X's?) chauffeur. The chauffeur glared at Honeybath. Honeybath, still on the ground, glared at him. And then the man turned and vanished.

'Are you badly hurt?' Diana Mariner was bending over him.

'No, not badly.' It was by some mysterious intuition that Honeybath knew this. 'But get the police. Get the police, after all. I've been murdered. I mean, I've been – ' Honeybath was incoherent.

'Can you get up?' Miss Mariner was less concerned than peremptory. 'This place just isn't healthy. Get into the car. We'll beat it before the fuss starts.'

Not unnaturally, this wouldn't have been easy. In fact, a fuss *was* starting. One or two people had paused near by, and were staring in the passive and unready way into which unexpected exigency tends to precipitate modern urban man. But from a little further off there came more purposive shouts, and Honeybath fancied he glimpsed a couple of uniformed men who might be either railway officials or policemen. By this time, however, he had actually been bundled into the Mini – a process making him aware that, if not hurt in the sense of being a mass of broken bones, he was certainly going to find himself atrociously bruised all over. The Mini was in motion, and he knew this to be quite wrong. Even if one has been only at the most sheerly receiving end of an accident, one certainly mustn't bolt from it. One explains things to a constable, gives one's name and address, is dusted down and handed one's umbrella or whatever by sympathetic persons. One –

He realized his mind was wandering. He hadn't been involved in an accident. *They had tried to murder him.* Perhaps the girl felt that a second attempt might follow at any moment. Yes – this must be why she was hurrying him from the scene.

He was conscious of being glad it was happening that way, but he didn't at all know why. Then in an instant he did know why. Since childhood he had owned an irrational fear of hospitals and nursing homes, and what he chiefly associated street accidents with was the horror of suddenly finding oneself being borne away to such a place in a hideously ululating ambulance. Even if nothing much had happened to you, they snatched you up, hurtled you dangerously through the traffic, decanted you into a casualty ward, and treated you for shock – whatever that might be. He didn't believe in shock, and from this it logically followed that he didn't believe in treatment for it either. So it was just as well that this remarkable young woman had taken such decisive action.

The Mini cornered so sharply that Honeybath was bumped against its side, and thus abruptly made aware that his numbed body would soon be aching all over. He was also made aware that his mind wasn't working very well, and even that something physical seemed to be happening inside his head. Had he, perhaps, suffered a stroke? Was cerebral disaster of some sort a common concomitant of such an accident as he had just suffered? Would he presently develop a blinding headache, and be dead in the morning?

But there hadn't been an accident. *They had tried to murder him.* As this fact came back to Honeybath he understood that what was building up inside his skull was nothing more sinister than a large and legitimate indignation. And it wasn't so much the attempt itself as its utterly unaccountable character that outraged him. He had done his job for these people (and thoroughly inexplicable the job, for a start, had been), and they had then merely turfed him out contemptuously, with his money in his pocket. Now – only minutes ago – they had done their best to pound him to a pulp between a lorry and a brick wall.

Perhaps it was simply spite. The bank robbery had failed, and it was conceivable they knew it to have been through his instrumentality that this had happened and that Crumble had been caught. They were simply determined to get their own back. That was it. Or rather it wasn't – Honeybath's perturbed mind abruptly contradicted itself – since professional criminals don't work that way. They don't go in for vengeance, or if they do so it is only between themselves. They had tried to eliminate him because they knew he was on their track. They must have been trailing him wherever he went. One of them must have been on the train, and tumbled to the significance of his sheaf of maps. Perhaps even the extraordinary coincidence of his encountering Diana Mariner and conversing with her had been a point that had instantly got home. And at Swindon some swift signal had been given –

Charles Honeybath shivered. (Since he was in fact in a state of shock which any ambulance man would have identified instantly, this was natural enough.) Had he bitten off more than he could chew? He had certainly got into deep water – and for the moment, at least, it felt uncommonly icy water as well. And it was sink or swim now. For he wasn't going back. He wasn't, for example, going to insist on being taken straight to the nearest police station, where he might contact Keybird and be placed under adequate protection until the whole affair was cleared up. On the contrary, he was going to go straight ahead.

And he had, after all, enjoyed one enormous piece of luck. Had Arbuthnot's tenancy (or Colonel Bunbury's tenancy) not expired when it had, and had he rediscovered the place of his late incarceration on his own, he might have plunged in with a stupid hardihood which could have been fatal. As it was, the respectable Admiral Mariner was in front of him and the resourceful and beautiful Diana Mariner was at his side. Imlac House would no longer be a prison. It would be a fresh base for a decisive move against the villains.

This was a comforting thought. Because comforting, it was relaxing. Honeybath felt tension drain out of him. Just for the moment, he need badger his brains no more. He closed his eyes; he shivered again; and, as usual, he fell asleep.

16

'And here we are,' Diana Mariner said.

'Yes, of course.' Honeybath jerked this reply out of himself. He wasn't sure whether it was the girl's voice or the distant sound of a railway-train that had roused him from some obscurely stupefied condition; both hung momentarily on his ear now. 'So we are.'

'Then you recognize the house?' Miss Mariner seemed gratified that this should be so.

'Not exactly.' Honeybath looked vaguely at what appeared to be a modern wing added to the large Georgian mansion. 'You see, from the garden –'

'Yes, I see. This is just our family *Lebensraum* at this end. They'll have been putting the rest in mothballs until there's another tenant. I say, can you get out?'

'Certainly I can get out.' Honeybath made a big effort, and did so. He found that he was quite steady on his feet, but that few joints in his body were much disposed to perform their normal offices without fuss. One painful movement brought him against the side of the Mini with a bump – and the bump produced a muffled clank. He remembered the bizarre circumstance that he had a revolver in his coat-pocket. He wondered whether such weapons ever discharged themselves accidentally. Something of the kind might well have happened when he was struck that glancing blow by the lethal lorry. If one had been a soldier one would understand these things. He had not.

'And here is Daddy,' Miss Mariner said. 'Won't this be a surprise for him?'

It showed no sign of being anything of the sort. A grey-haired and distinguished-looking man had indeed appeared in a doorway. But it was at once clear that if Miss Mariner chose to decant from her car a dusty, dazed and crumpled stranger, that stranger would instantly be received as a guest, and without flicker, by Miss Mariner's father.

'I am so very glad to meet you,' Admiral Mariner said, and shook hands. His tone was properly formal; he wasn't in the least suggesting that his words should be taken literally; they were to be construed in some such sense as 'You seem a perfectly reasonable chap and I don't at all mind offering you a cup of tea.' Honeybath approved of this. He felt secure with Admiral Mariner. It was odd that the Admiral should be an ambassador. Presumably it was to some predominantly maritime power.

'Mr Honeybath is the portrait-painter,' Miss Mariner said.

'How very interesting.' The Admiral's manner of saying this was highly commendatory; he was acknowledging not only his guest's known eminence but also the propriety with which his daughter had signalled it by her employment of the definite article. Honeybath was further comforted. He was sensitive to subtleties of this kind. 'If I may say so,' the Admiral added, 'I look out for your work every year.'

'Thank you very much.' This further civility clearly referred to the Royal Academy's annual jamboree at Burlington House. Honeybath received it gratefully.

'That supermarket fellow who calls himself – what is it? – Lord President of the Council. To my mind, you had him to a T. And – talking of tea – come on in.'

This, to Honeybath's mind, was highly felicitous. Mariner actually *did* have his work in his head. He had proved it by the lightest of allusions. And then he had added that small, unassuming joke.

'I'd like some tea very much,' Honeybath said. 'I come to you – and wholly through your daughter's kindness – after rather an unnerving adventure.' He was keeping his end up. 'It's why I need a clothes-brush first.'

'As you certainly do, my dear sir.' Mariner allowed himself to be sympathetically amused. 'But has there been an accident? You're not hurt? Our GP lives no distance away. Send for him in a moment.'

'No, no – only a bruise or two.'

'Mr Honeybath has been pretty lucky,' Miss Mariner said. 'They tried to murder him.'

'What's that?' Mere urbanity dropped away from Admiral Mariner. He was instantly alert and formidable. It was evident that he could trust his daughter not to be merely silly. 'Who are *they*, my dear?'

'Daddy, I think you ought to prepare yourself for a shock. It looks as if your Colonel Bunbury was not what he appeared to be.'

'Bunbury?' Just for a second, Admiral Mariner was at a loss. 'But, yes – of course. I've been doing my best to drive the fellow out of my head. And precisely because I've been suspecting there was something damned fishy about him. Mr Honeybath, tea will be ready by the time you've had a wash.'

If tea was no great success, the fault wasn't the Mariners'. There were still only the two of them, so that Honeybath conjectured that the Admiral must be a widower. They both worked hard, and on the principle of refreshment first and serious talk later. But Honeybath found his shivering fits coming back to him, and the clink of a tea-spoon could make him jump. Being upset in this way because of his near shave infuriated him; he had always cherished a myth of himself as inwardly quite a tough character. He still believed it to be true that in a crisis he would stand up and be counted. But at the moment he was behaving like an old wife. It was only when tea gave place to brandy – this through some unobtrusive exercise of tact on the Admiral's part – that he really found his tongue. And, when he did so, it was with awkward abruptness.

'Has everything gone?' he asked. 'Everything that was in any sense those people's property, I mean. For example, my portrait.'

'Your portrait?' Admiral Mariner was perplexed. 'They had a portrait of you? How very odd!'

'Daddy, do think.' For the first time, Diana hinted impatience with her parent. 'You *know* Mr Honeybath *paints* portraits. He came to Imlac to paint one. But not, it seems, of Colonel Bunbury. And he's anxious about it. It was got out of him, I think, by a kind of fraud. He wants to get it back.'

'It isn't likely they've left anything of the kind behind them.' Admiral Mariner thought for a moment, and then distinguishably hesitated, as if before a delicate point. 'Unless, of course – and I haven't yet got the hang of the thing at all – unless the painting of a portrait was a mere pretext for detaining Mr Honeybath at Imlac, and they simply shoved it aside when it had served its turn. If there's any possibility of that sort, we had better hunt through the whole house. But it will take some time. If I might just be told – '

'Yes, of course.' And Honeybath took a deep breath (followed by a little more brandy) and told his story. He found it hard to organize at first, even although he had a sense of his own mind as clearing rapidly. It isn't easy to render lucid an account of matters which have to be admitted as in essence inexplicable. But at least he had the advantage of an attentive auditory. The Admiral might well have felt that he was suffering politely a narrative of absurd events his own implication with which was accidental and a matter of mere bad luck. But in fact he listened with what was plainly intense concentration throughout. Honeybath, who was professionally alert to small muscular movements, was conscious of both father and daughter, indeed, several times tautening as if before an expectation of crisis. Neither of them interrupted until he had finished. When he did so, it was to hear from the Admiral something like a long, gentle sigh, and to observe that he was somehow sitting more easily in his chair.

'You relieve me,' the Admiral said. 'A great deal of money has been stolen, and you yourself have been most outrageously treated. But at least nothing really horrible has occurred.'

'It nearly has,' Diana Mariner said. 'There in the railway yard.'

'Perfectly true.' Her father nodded soberly. 'The picture changes at that point. There is something almost engaging – you won't misunderstand me, Honeybath – about the ingenuity, almost the fantasy, of the main plot. But when the epilogue turns out to be attempted murder we have to take another view of the thing.'

'I'm not quite clear,' Honeybath said, 'about what was the main plot. The proportions of the thing disturb me. Renting this large house of yours for a long period, and putting up that whole sustained charade of the portrait-painting just to get me out of the way: I have an obstinate feeling that it doesn't make sense.'

'That's a most interesting idea. But we have to remember, I think, that half a million pounds is a very large sum of money indeed. It's a far richer prize than any half million pounds' worth of jewellery or paintings or anything of the kind. You can't part with stolen goods without losing heavily – whereas, stolen or unstolen banknotes are worth precisely what they say they are. And there's another thing. Bunbury's tenancy ended just after the robbery went through as planned. That's a strong argument that the whole set-up has been in aid of the bank raid and nothing else. Don't you agree?'

'I don't know that I do. But the police certainly take that view.' For the first time since the attack on him, Honeybath managed a smile. 'They just couldn't be less interested in my poor Mr X.'

'Well, I differ from them there.' Mariner, as if sensitive to his guest's slightest change of mood, produced a quiet chuckle. 'I find him quite fascinating – although in rather a macabre way. Did you bring away any sketches of him?'

'None at all. Of course, I made a number – and actually gave him several. He was good enough to say he'd deposit them in the imperial archives.'

'He studied them – even handled them a good deal?'

'Oh, certainly. Sat on them too, as a matter of fact.'

'How very amusing.' Mariner glanced at his daughter, as if requiring her to be amused also. 'But there must have been a pathetic side to the thing. Was it your impression that the poor fellow's mind was hopelessly darkened?'

'Yes. Short of his being a superb actor, it was definitely that.'

'He was Napoleon *tout simple*? I mean, he never seemed to have an inkling of being anybody else?'

'I wouldn't quite say that.'

'Ah!' Admiral Mariner might have been a mental specialist absorbed in the particulars of a case, so sharply did this exclamation escape him. 'He had lucid periods?'

'No, I don't think they could be called that. It was just that he seemed to have other, and much more fragmentary, fantasies. He seemed to believe that he had once been in gaol.'

'I don't know that that one sounds too unlikely,' Miss Mariner said crisply. 'Not considering the company he appears to have been keeping. A gang of criminals swarming all over Imlac! I keep on finding it hard to believe.'

'The alternative, my dear Miss Mariner, is to believe me very much dottier than the Napoleonic Mr X.' Honeybath told himself that he must have recovered his customary poise in order to make possible this good-humoured remark. 'And I'm bound to say I've had moments when I've wondered about myself.'

'As we all sometimes do.' It was presumably the ambassadorial Mariner who offered this tactful comment.

'I take it that Mr X's mental incapacity is immediately apparent? He isn't the kind of person who would be believed by a jury, or anything of that kind?'

'Most decidedly not.'

'It's really a most perplexing affair. Presently I must tell you whatever I know about Bunbury – if Bunbury is really his name, which is something we must now be disposed to doubt.' Mariner glanced at his watch. 'But dear me! I see that it is almost dinner time. You will, of course, dine with us, Honeybath? Indeed, it is plain that you must consent to stay the night at Imlac. Do not think me impertinent if I say that you are already rather plainly in need of bed.'

'I really feel – '

'Diana will simply not take a refusal from you, my dear sir. We'll dine, talk briefly of other things, and in the morning sally into the house.' Mariner made a vaguely expansive gesture. 'If your portrait has been abandoned anywhere, we shall find it. And then we must consider the next step. I think it involves your acquaintance in those higher reaches of the metropolitan police. But we shall see.'

This programme fulfilled itself (or at least the first part of it did). There was nothing overbearing about Diana Mariner's father. (Admirals can run on an overbearing ticket, but not ambassadors.) Yet he was a man who seemed quite naturally to get his own way. He was also so shrewd a character that Honeybath wondered how he could have been taken in by Arbuthnot-Bunbury as a tenant. Neither about this nor about anything else, however, did he wonder consistently or for long. Telling his own alarming story had exhausted the small store of regained energy brandy had built up, and he did very much want to get to bed. He was abominably aching all over. It was a condition, reason told him, which would get worse rather than better on the following day. But mere animal instinct prompted him to crawl away and rest in the interim.

The Mariners appeared to have carved themselves out a sort of maisonette in this part of the house. It was unassuming but surprisingly roomy, and adequate services were laid on. A respectable elderly female produced a respectable dinner, and the Admiral played his part by opening a bottle of claret which was distinctly on the notable side of merely sound. He also put up just the right amount of unexacting conversation on general topics. Honeybath judged this giving a rest to mystery, murder and criminality a properly civilized thing. When, thus soothed, he went to bed (in borrowed pyjamas) he expected to fall asleep at once.

He only drowsed. Two or three times, and as if from rather far away, he heard a passing train. He wondered how his present bedroom lay in relation to his place of incarceration only a few days before. Probably the whole bulk of the main house interposed between him and the park and railway-line. The familiar church or stable bell sounded, and he was surprised that it was only eleven o'clock; in his hazy state he supposed himself to have reached the small hours. The bed was comfortable – an important point in his battered state – and he now resigned himself to a more or less sleepless night. An inspection of his person with the aid of a couple of looking-glasses (an unfamiliar exercise, since he had no narcissistic impulses) had suggested to him already that he had perhaps been exaggerating his injuries. He was a trifle soft, after all. And he now discovered that there were various ways in which the slight moving of a limb beneath the bedclothes could afford him an ease which brought a sensation of almost positive pleasure.

Then – and quite suddenly – his body, thus variously relaxed, agonizingly stiffened. For a moment the sensation was of a hideously pervasive cramp. Had some vital nerve centre within himself, weakened by that dreadful blow, now abruptly given way? Was he going to be paralysed for the remainder of his days? Would he ever be able to paint again?

Cautiously, he tried out the several attachments to his person: left leg, right leg, left arm, and then – crucially – right arm. Everything remained in working order. He realized that the only happening had been inside his head. And he became aware of just what that happening had been.

But it couldn't, of course, be. His attention had wandered. Or memory – very short-term memory indeed – was playing a malicious prank on him. *Of course* he had heard –

He lay quite still in the darkness of his strange room, and the long minutes drained away. There was nothing to do but wait, and he refrained even from turning on the bedside lamp and looking at his watch. He was visited by the strange fancy of having been submerged in a comfortably hot bath the level of which was now very slowly sinking, so that he was being progressively exposed to a bleakly chill air. Certainly his body was growing cold. He felt the wintry grip of what he was afraid must be fear; felt it in his most vital parts.

Midnight struck – and now there could be no doubt of it. The ninth stroke had been precisely like its fellows. And so it had been an hour earlier. Neither sense nor memory had betrayed him.

But his own wits had. Confused by that hideous blow, he had let himself be monstrously imposed upon. *This was not Imlac House.*

PART FOUR

THE TWINS

17

Charles Honeybath faced it coldly – coldly in the sense that he still felt that nasty chill, but coldly also as being now capable of dispassionate and objective appraisal. He told himself that at least he seemed to be through with funk. For the second time within three weeks he was in a monstrous and inexplicable situation. And the challenge to his intelligence of these reduplicated inexplicabilities had suddenly become so imperative that being scared had somehow revealed itself as a waste of time. He heard himself (to his own surprise) laugh aloud in the darkness. He put out a hand and turned on the light.

He nipped out of bed. He did this, for the moment, without any sense that he was a bag of bruises. He tiptoed swiftly and silently to the door of the room. There was a key in the lock. He turned it, and went back to bed. At least he couldn't be surprised by assassins now. Unless, of course, they set the whole place on fire, or something like that.

He knew why he had been taken to the real Imlac. It had been to paint the portrait of an elderly lunatic. That had been a *genuine* reason. He felt sure of this. The commission hadn't been an arbitrarily chosen means of getting and keeping him out of the way, as in some Sherlock Holmes story he'd once read. It had been at the heart of the matter – whatever the matter was. Honeybath wasn't quite clear why he felt so certain of this. But he did feel certain of it. Of course the commission *had* resulted in his being absent from his studio for a fortnight; and it was undeniable that it was that absence which had made the bank robbery feasible. But the bank robbery had been a sideline: a subsidiary operation suddenly glimpsed in the course of planning something quite different. Perhaps the bank robbery represented Peach more or less out on his own; it had just been an inspiration that had come to him when securing Honeybath's services for the portrait of Mr X. He might have got an OK from his bosses and then contacted a suitable gang of safe-busters or whatever they were called.

So shove the bank robbery out of your head, Honeybath enjoined himself at this stage. You were taken to Imlac to paint that weird old man. And you have been brought *here* – which isn't Imlac at all – as a totally unaccountable sequel. It's your job to make sense of it.

These people, the Mariners, have told you an outrageous pack of lies. Including, no doubt, the statement that their name is Mariner. It isn't. Peach's name has proved not to be Peach, Arbuthnot's is assuredly not Arbuthnot or Bunbury either, and nobody has pretended that Mr X has X as a bizarre but authentic surname. Presumably Keybird is Keybird, and I possess a birth certificate confirming that I am Honeybath. But any certainty of nomenclature stops just there.

I know – he repeated to himself – why I was taken to Imlac House. Or at least I can identify what a philosopher would term a proximate cause. But why have I been lured *here*? Unless they propose to murder and bury me on the spot, it looks to have been a pretty expensive operation. Here is another large house – although not necessarily so large as Imlac – in the ownership, or at least the tenancy of this bogus Admiral of the Fleet. They are treating it as expendable merely in the interest of their little confabulation with me. I can't leave this place without *knowing* that it isn't Imlac. But it can't be far from Imlac. As soon as I get free, I'm bound to go back to the police, and within hours they'll have identified this house and investigated it. And whatever the Mariners are about certainly won't stand up to *that.* So they'll have beaten it – just as by this time Arbuthnot and his crowd will almost certainly have beaten it from the real Imlac. So what have the Mariners been after?

On the train he had been foolishly communicative with the girl, so that she had rapidly been able to place him in the context of something she knew a great deal about. She would have been able to telephone her father (if he was her father) while away all that time on the pretext of hunting for her Mini; she would have done that, and so put him in the picture against their arrival half an hour later at this house. But, meanwhile, her having contacted Honeybath had been observed – and the attempt to murder him had been the prompt sequel.

What hove into view – Honeybath suddenly understood – was *two rival criminal organizations*. He could think of just nothing else that so much as began to provide an intelligible framework for the sequence of events in which he had been implicated.

He rested for a moment on this startling hypothesis. It gave his present situation an uncommonly unhealthy look. He decidedly hadn't got himself mixed up with small-time crooks. Rather he might be described as between the fell incensed points of mighty opposites. And if the one lot had been perfectly prepared to flatten him out against a brick wall, it wasn't to be supposed that the other would be backward in thinking up some answering pleasantry if it in the least suited their convenience.

Honeybath paused on this discouraging reflection to listen intently. They had got him off to bed, and might by now be supposing that he was fast asleep. It was true that he had locked what appeared to be the only entrance to the room. But might it not run to a trapdoor, or something of that kind? What about the bed's being so constructed that, at the touch of a distant lever, it would vanish through the floor? What about a deadly snake crawling down a bell-rope? It was true there didn't seem to be a bell-rope – but in a large way the possibility held, all the same. For the point was – and he saw this with immense clarity – that they had now got what they wanted from him. Indefinably but beyond cavil – this was just a sudden retrospective revelation – his teatime colloquy with the Mariners had concluded on a note of something like relaxation and ease. They had, those two, as it were, coaxed the cat out of the bag.

So just what had he told them that they hadn't known? They had of course pretended that he had been the bearer of staggering revelation all along the line. Mariner's audacity in representing his abode to be Imlac House, and himself as having let it to a tenant whose criminal courses were utterly unsuspected by him, made this plain sailing. Yet there had been, so to speak, ever so many hidden rocks; and it simply amazed Honeybath now that he had not in one way or another tumbled to the fact that he was being submitted to a gross and ramshackle deception.

What, *not* known to them, had they been going after?

The fullest information about Mr X. Surely that was it! Honeybath paused on this. He had the mystery, he told himself, by the tip of its tail – but it would elude him if he didn't make one further grab. Very well. That was wrong. Mariner *hadn't* gone after what might be called the full portrait of Mr X. There were things which it would have been natural to ask which he hadn't asked. It was almost as if he had forgotten that he was supposed to know nothing about the mysterious invalid at all. And what he *had* wanted was something like precise particulars of that invalidism itself. Just what was the degree – it might be styled the reliable degree – of Mr X's imbecility? It was when Mariner gained a fairly definitive answer on that one that his attention had relaxed, and Honeybath had been politely packed off to bed.

He was in bed now – and it wasn't the right place for him. The time was well past one o'clock. But he ought to be up and doing, all the same.

This was a curious persuasion, and perhaps there can be no wholly convincing explanation of it. The fact that he had worked out at least part of the puzzle, had a little pushed back the frontier of mystification, possibly acted upon him as an intellectual irritant. The remaining parts of the enigma he was now going to take by the throat. And he would begin by extracting any information he could from this offensively spurious house. The enterprise might be dangerous. But he possessed, if it came to a pinch, a weapon much more accurately lethal than a reversing lorry. The wretched Peach's revolver was still in his coat-pocket, and the coat was flung over a chair close to his bed.

He got up and dressed stealthily – looking round, as he did so, for anything else that might he useful. It was a well-appointed bedroom. There was provision for making himself tea. There was a tin of biscuits. There were candles on the dressing-table. There was also the electric torch which the inability of England's Electricity Boards to survive mild atmospheric disturbance in rural areas constrains all prudent householders to provide by every bedside. Honeybath picked it up and tested it. If anything, the beam was too bright and clear. He would have preferred that paradoxically named object, a dark lantern, with which he recalled the heroes of juvenile fiction as having been frequently equipped long ago. Still, the torch would serve. If the bogus Admiral, the fraudulent Ambassador (how *could* he for a moment have believed such rubbish?) revealed himself suddenly in its glare, that would be just too bad.

Dressed and equipped, Honeybath unlocked the bedroom door, opened it, and stepped into the corridor. His romantic side was in control, and he suddenly felt thoroughly dangerous. In his head, indeed, was the image of a lean grey cruiser silently slipping its moorings and melting into the night.

18

At least he was at sea. He knew almost nothing about what surrounded him. The house he had glimpsed on arrival was certainly a substantial mansion of respectable antiquity, and he had so far been in no more than a kind of independent wing or annex added at a later date. The girl calling herself Diana Mariner had said something implying that, when not actually let, the main house remained untenanted – this since her father, even when at home, was constrained to a modest manner of life. But Honeybath could now believe no word that he had been told by these people. If he managed to penetrate to the main house (where his instinct for exploration lay), there was no valid reason for believing that it would in fact prove to be deserted. The Mariners themselves might have retreated to it, for all he knew.

He switched on his torch, and crept downstairs. There was an element of irrationality in this, since the light was almost as likely to betray him as was any slight noise he might make. He had no choice in the matter, however, since it would be impossible to move at all in mere darkness. But he arrived without misadventure in a small square hall which he remembered pretty well. In one wall there was only the outer door by which he had arrived, flanked by a window on either hand. The walls on either side each showed a couple of doors. On the fourth side there was only one door, centrally placed, and it was distinguished from all the others by being covered in green baize. It might well lead to kitchens and the like, but he took a guess that it in fact represented a means of communication with the main dwelling. He pulled it cautiously open, and found that it then remained in this position of its own accord. But what his torch now further revealed was the perplexing appearance of a perfectly smooth wall. He put his free hand on this and moved it over the surface. The result was a strong impression that what confronted him was a sheet of steel.

Just what he thought of this was not clear to Honeybath, but his immediate action was to move to one of the windows. Rather in the fashion he had employed when the involuntary guest of Mr Basil Arbuthnot, he slipped behind a curtain and peered out. Or, to be more exact, he thought to peer out, and was arrested by the disconcerting circumstance that interposed between himself and the external world there was something less vulnerable than a mere pane of glass. There was a fine steel lattice as well. He was in a prison. Or if he wasn't in a prison he was in a fortress. There seemed to he no means of telling which.

He let the torch play round the hall again. It was furnished with a restrained elegance wholly inapposite in the light of this grim discovery. On the floor lay a couple of Persian rugs which would certainly realize in a saleroom enough to stock several large cellars with the kind of claret with which he had been regaled at dinner. The few pieces of furniture had begun life in France some centuries ago. On delicate pedestals round the walls stood small bronzes which at once spoke to his trained sense of the Italy of the *cinquecento*. The place was certainly no thieves' kitchen. Honeybath was astonished that he hadn't become aware of its respectable opulence before. He wondered fleetingly whether one of those falling bricks hadn't hit him on the head. He must certainly have been in a fairly witless condition earlier that night.

And this thought had an almost immediate physical effect. He had gone back to the door that wasn't a door, and was playing the torch anew on its blank surface, when a momentary giddiness overtook him. He put out a hand to steady himself, and became aware to his horror that he had grasped one of the delicate bronzes. It moved and was almost certainly going to fall with a crash to the floor. Only it didn't fall; it simply twisted oddly in his grasp. And at once the smooth sheet of white-painted steel moved silently sideways and vanished.

There was a dark corridor in front of him.

In fact, the place *was* a fortress – that rather than a simple fort. Stronghold within stronghold was the principle upon which it had been constructed. It was probably a much more efficient and imaginatively resourceful job than that confounded London bank.

Charles Honeybath had a momentary sense (which may be excused him) of having drastically misestimated his situation. In the environment that bad been disclosing itself to him during the past few minutes the fearsome and unfamiliar weapon in his pocket (which he had only the most general notion of how to discharge at an adversary) shrank in potential effectiveness to the dimensions of a pea-shooter. If at any moment lights snapped on and some challenge rang out it would probably be as the prelude to a burst of automatic fire of the kind that riddles one with bullets in two seconds flat. He possessed only hazy notions of organized crime. But he knew that it existed in England on a scale undreamed of a generation or even a decade ago, and that it had its High Commands as certainly as had the armed forces of the Crown. And this was the headquarters of one of them. It was to be likened to one of those comfortable chateaux from which, in the great European wars of the present century, invisible armies had been directed by generals drawing inspiration from claret even better than that commanded by Admiral Mariner. The Admiral was such a general. Mr Basil Arbuthnot was another – and on the opposing side.

Honeybath recognized as he stood that this was a highly coloured and indeed almost apocalyptic vision. But he hadn't a doubt of its validity. The only question was what he himself could now do about it. What he did was to draw the revolver from his pocket, direct the beam of his torch straight down the corridor, and march ahead at a brisk pace. The gesture might have been called Honeybath's Reply.

He was in another square hall. It was much larger than the one behind him, but much barer as well. The original architect, indeed, had thought a little to soften the bleakly rectangular effect by creating in each corner niches apparently designed for the reception of life-size statues of one sort or another. But the niches stood empty, and were thus somehow of curiously sinister effect. The only furnishing consisted of a couple of large but shallow cupboards ranged against two of the walls. He strode over to one of these and pulled open a door. What was revealed was a row of rifles of some sort in a rack. There was a wicked gleam to them which was wholly displeasing, and he shut the door again abruptly. He understood that he was in an armoury. He understood, too, the significance of the cupboard's being unlocked. The house itself was an impenetrable stronghold, so that no further security was needed. Only it was a security which had been breached. By Charles Honeybath RA. And a strange possibility occurred to him. The remaining secrets of the place might well be disposed on, so to speak, an open-access principle. He had only to poke around, and all would be revealed to him.

If, of course, his investigations were suffered to proceed uninterrupted. Was the house a mere depository, and untenanted at least by night? Were the Mariners in their contiguous dwelling its only guardians? This would be a rash bet. As in a museum or picture gallery there would surely be some nocturnal patrol: a watchman, or watchmen, charged with the duty of perambulating the building and systematically checking up.

He supposed that he could retreat. He could return through that ominous steel valve, manipulate the bronze that would seal it anew, creep back to his room, and hope in the morning to break out from the damnable place, if necessary at the point of his suddenly flourished pistol. This would be his rational course. The house could not be at all that distance from other human habitation. Just get to a telephone, and it would be all up with his enemies. Or might he, here and now, find a telephone and dial that attractive 999? But then he had no notion where he was – so how could the forces of the law be rapidly brought to his aid? What about trying to burn the place down? A really hearty conflagration would probably bring along a fire brigade in no time at all.

For some seconds Honeybath stood immobile but not irresolute – like the Homeric hero hither and thither dividing the swift mind. He asked himself in what interest he had really embarked on his hare-brained expedition. The answer was that confounded portrait. He wanted the portrait – more badly than almost anything he had ever wanted before. If what he had achieved had been to penetrate into the genuine Imlac House there would be an outside chance of its being within his grasp. But there was not the slightest reason to suppose that it had found a resting-place in *this* house, or that the obscure purposes for which it had been commissioned had anything whatever to do with the so-called Mariners. It was Mr X himself in whom, for some reason, they were interested, and not the masterpiece which Charles Honeybath had achieved by setting up his canvas before him. So the Mariners and their mysterious criminal empire were a side-issue, so far as he was concerned. A single honest look at himself told him that he had no genuine passion for simply apprehending crooks. Still, he wanted to *know*. So he wasn't turning back before taking, at least, a further look round.

Two corridors, several doors, a handsome staircase: he could take his choice. If there were people sleeping in the house it would presumably be on an upper storey. So perhaps he ought to go upstairs first, and find cautious means to satisfy himself on this point. He could creep from door to door, listening for the faint suspirations of slumbering persons and then peering into every room in turn. The result, if wholly negative, might relieve his mind and encourage him to explore this ground floor at leisure. But such a choice would surely be laborious, time-consuming, and hazardous. It would be better boldly to tackle his immediate surroundings first. Deciding thus, Honeybath advanced to the nearest door and opened it.

'*Turn off that bloody light!*'

The words had come to him out of the darkness ahead in a hiss at once so apprehensive and commanding that Honeybath snapped off his torch at once. The injunction had been surprising, if only because it was precisely not a challenge. But, whatever it portended, momentary darkness was his best resource. A man with a blazing torch in his hand is a sitting target, after all.

'There are three of them up there tonight, you flaming fool.' The voice now came not from complete obscurity but from a region in which there could just be distinguished a dull red glow. Here, in fact, was another prowler, and one more discreetly accommodated with an aid to vision. The glow brightened a very little, as if upon the cautious manipulation of a shutter upon what might be called a very dark lantern indeed. 'Where are the rest of you?' the voice hissed. 'All safe inside yet?'

'Not yet.' Honeybath found that he had summoned up a hoarse whisper. 'One at a time – that's the order. Do you think we all want to risk falling into a bloody trap at once? We're trusting you just as far as we have to, aren't we? What do you take us for, mate?'

To this speech, certainly the most brilliant he had ever uttered, Honeybath had been assisted by another Homeric reference. The man in the darkness was Sinon, and he himself was the first Greek to emerge from the Trojan Horse. Roughly, the situation was that. But only, perhaps, very roughly. Put it, rather, that the Mariners' fortress was under siege; that here was a fifth-column character who had been suborned to open the gate; and that he, Honeybath, had talked himself into the role of the vanguard of the invading force. Unfortunately it was necessary to believe that there *was* an invading force, and that it was due to turn up at any time. Just how long had he got for manoeuvre before this occurred? Honeybath had barely formulated the unspoken question before it was miraculously answered.

'The bloody synchronization's haywire,' the voice from the darkness said. 'Another twenty minutes, it should be, before you bastards turn up. I've still got my trip-wires to set.'

'Have you, indeed?' As his eyes accommodated themselves to the faint light, Honeybath began to distinguish the figure and features of the false Sinon. He was between young and very young, he was weedy,

149

and it was possible to sense that he was acutely apprehensive as well. It would probably pay off to take a bold line with the chap. 'Then get on with it,' he said briskly, 'and don't waste any more of my time. Careful about it, too. If I hear you make a sound, I'll come and throttle you.'

'OK, OK.' The young man was at once sullen and alarmed. 'No need to get nasty.'

'Then get cracking. But one moment! Which is the room with those bloody records?'

'The files, you mean?' The young man seemed puzzled. 'All that dossier stuff?'

'You know very well what I mean. It's part of what we're here for, isn't it?'

'I don't know what you're here for.' The young man was sulky. 'But I know there will be blue murder if it goes wrong. And what you seem to be after is in the next room. But I reckon most of it will be in the safe they have in there. A six-hour job. I'd say that would be.'

'I'm not interested in what'd you'd say. Clear out, son – see?'

19

It had been as easy as that, Honeybath told himself. He was alone in the next room. The weedy youth had departed to his trip-wires – which were presumably to constitute some booby-trap when the night's work really got going. Why were the self-denominated Mariners and the small bunch of thugs they appeared to keep in this house going to be robbed or raided or massacred or whatever it was? Honeybath hadn't a clue. And then – suddenly – he *had* a clue. It was because the Mariners were entertaining (or had kidnapped) Charles Honeybath RA. Arbuthnot and Co. (who so clearly constituted the rival gang) knew that this coup had brought about some crisis. And to this crisis they proposed, within the next twenty minutes, to produce a violent and devastating response.

But what did Arbuthnot know that the bogus Admiral must by now have extracted from Honeybath? Could it be the tie-up with Peach-Crumble and the bank raid? Could it be the mere existence and location of the Arbuthnot headquarters at Imlac House? Could it be another mere existence: the mere existence of Mr X? This last was the best guess, Honeybath told himself. But it still wasn't quite good enough.

The lunacy of Mr X. Not his existence, but his *lunacy*. That was it. He had already *seen* that that was it, but in a dark and cloudy fashion. The point was clear to him now. Because the Mariners knew that Mr X was hopelessly *non compos mentis* the Arbuthnots had lost a trick. They were about to play their next card.

Honeybath turned on the light and switched off his torch. He had no time for groping around; anything that was to be discovered must be discovered now. Moreover he was gaining in confidence. Irrationally perhaps, he saw himself as a kind of third force – or even as what the learned would call a *tertius gaudens*, meaning a chap who nips in and does both contending sides down. It was no doubt a sober possibility that the contending sides would combine together for long enough to do *him* down. But he would take a gamble on that.

If the hall had been bleak, this room was bleaker. It might have been described as a cross between an office and a laboratory. The illumination he had switched on came from long tubes sited near the ceiling and so disposed as to cast a cold shadowless glare. There were desks and benches, and a great many chests and cupboards all of which proved to be locked. The safe looked very aggressively safe, and of course it was locked too. So much for his notion that, within the fortress, there would be no internal security.

The whole place, moreover, was depressingly tidy, swept, and ungarnished. No exotic cigarette-stubs in ashtrays, no revelatory photographs on walls. Everything put away. Or everything except a single litter of books and papers on a small table in a corner. He moved over to this. It didn't take him long to recognize something. In fact he found himself looking at one of his own sketches of Mr X. It was in part dusted over with a fine grey powder.

Charles Honeybath (seasoned private investigator) hadn't a moment's doubt about the significance of this. It didn't even surprise him. He remembered how Peach had jumped at the fact that there would be preparatory sketches of Mr X, and had made sure that Mr X would be let handle them and retain them. Mr X *had* so done, before firmly sitting on the things as a preliminary to depositing them in the imperial archives. They must have the poor old chap's fingerprints all over them. And these fingerprints somebody had been industriously recovering.

What did surprise Honeybath was the two fat volumes that lay open on the desk. They were like outsize family photograph albums.

They *were* photograph albums, and both were open upon a face Honeybath knew well. It was a face that had changed a good deal since either of these photographs was taken. The Mr X here commemorated was a much younger man. What presumably hadn't changed were his fingerprints. And there they – or rather his thumb-prints were: a pair to each photograph, and very neatly done. A professional job, in fact. So here was a different kind of archive: not imperial, but criminological. They must have just this sort of thing filed away by the thousand in that place at New Scotland Yard. It seemed crooks kept such records too.

But that wasn't all. Each of the photographs appeared on the left-hand side of an opening. On the right-hand side was a closely typed dossier. Honeybath knew at a glance that it could be nothing but that. Unfortunately there was little more to be learnt from it. Both dossiers were in some sort of code. But not entirely. Each concluded with what appeared to be a hastily scribbled pencil annotation. Under the first he read:

Old B. Oct. 1956

and under the second:

Pensioned Valparaiso Jan. 1957.

Cautiously – first in the one album and then in the other – Honeybath turned over a page or two. At every opening, the same general appearance. Rogues and their histories. As the sergeant in that rural police station would have said: Well, well, well. He turned back to his familiar acquaintance. *Pensioned Valparaiso Jan. 1957* seemed self-explanatory, more or less. No doubt you got honourably rid of an unwanted confederate in that considerate way. But what about *Old B. Oct. 1956?* An explanation started up in Honeybath's mind like a creation. *Old B.* stood for *Old Bailey*. In that month of that year one of Her Majesty's Judges had dealt faithfully with Mr X

– that much younger Mr X – in that dreaded citadel of the criminal law.

But it didn't make sense. A crook whose career closed on such a note one autumnal day in 1956 would be in no position to depart for South America on a winter day three months later. Honeybath considered this enigma – the two photographs, the two sets of thumbprints – resolutely at leisure. He had ceased to be bothered by the fact that twenty minutes is a brief space of time, and that now the final grains must pretty well be trickling through the glass.

It was only when he had solved the mystery – or at least glimpsed the large splendid outline of it – that he glanced at his watch.

What he had to do now was simply to get out. He hadn't found his portrait. But he felt his mission to be accomplished, all the same. And somewhere in this house the false Sinon had opened a door. And through a door by which many men might presently enter it ought to be possible for one man first to depart. Puzzle find the door, Honeybath said to himself – and walked back into the hall. It was in darkness. There wasn't even the weedy youth's silly little red lamp. Nevertheless Honeybath knew – having achieved some mysterious hyperacuity of sense – that the hall was full of men. Arbuthnot and Co. had arrived. All possibility of easy escape was over. Honeybath fished out the revolver – obscurely wondering whether it was at all legal, or even moral, to sell his life dearly. And then, suddenly, the hall was brilliantly illuminated.

'Mr Honeybath, this has been most injudicious behaviour on your part,' Detective Superintendent Keybird said.

20

'Ah, Mr Keybird, good morning to you.' Honeybath, who justly felt that his behaviour, whether injudicious or not, had been marked by at least some small measure of intrepidity, found himself indisposed to accept any note of censure. Of course one might have assumed that, in the situation in which he had landed himself, the unexpected arrival of the police in a big way would be wholly grateful to him. Hadn't he, no time ago, been wondering how to make that 999 call? There would have been nothing wholly out of the way in his now receiving Keybird and his legions with tears of joy.

But in fact – such is the mysterious obliquity and perversity of the human heart – Honeybath's predominant feeling was one of irritation. He had been doing very well. He had been (he fondly supposed) well ahead of the police – a whole street ahead, indeed, just as if he had been M. Poirot or Lord Peter Wimsey. But now here the police were, positively queering his pitch. It was extremely tiresome. He felt a sudden disposition to take the efficient Keybird on, as it were, the flank.

'May I ask,' he said blandly, 'whether you have yet found my portrait?'

'Found your portrait? No, I have not. But I have found you, Mr Honeybath. And I hope you'll consider that something to be going on with.'

'I'd rather you'd found the portrait, I confess. And I suppose you've cleaned up Imlac by now. Are you sure your men had a good rummage there?'

'Imlac?' The blank incomprehension with which Detective Superintendent Keybird repeated this word reflected an unwonted lack of wariness on his part.

'Imlac House. I take it you did begin there?'

'Mr Honeybath, I don't know what you are talking about.'

'Dear me!' It didn't escape Honeybath that he was behaving very badly. Sinon, in however distant a part of this nameless house he had been setting his booby traps, must by now be aware that there had arrived, so to speak, a Trojan Horse from quite the wrong stable. He would be changing sides again: alerting the three men whom he had spoken of as upstairs, and probably contriving to alert the Mariners as well. All these people might make a successful bolt for it while this Keybird comedy was going on. Or they might even launch some large-scale attack. But Honeybath disregarded these plain facts. The police, after all, were so numerously represented at this climactic scene that they could presumably look after themselves. 'Dear me!' he repeated. 'Then I can't understand quite why you should be here at all. It can't simply be that you've been following me around?'

'Do I imagine we *wouldn't* be following you around? You surely can't suppose, Mr Honeybath, that you're as yet all that in the clear? Come, come, sir!'

It was Honeybath's turn to be disconcerted. There was a short silence during which he became aware that the police posse was thinning out. Upon the instructions of some subordinate commander, he supposed, they were discreetly exploring the house. The curtain might go up – although on the Lord knew what – at any moment.

'Do I understand,' Honeybath asked, 'that you have been having me shadowed as a suspected person?'

'Under observation, sir, certainly. A routine proceeding in affairs of this sort.'

'A lot of good it did when they tried to murder me in that station yard.'

'Yes, sir. But it wasn't exactly protection we understood ourselves to be laying on. So our man was taken a little by surprise, I'm free to admit. But he did get the number of that Mini car. The subsequent inquiries took some time. I didn't myself get down until midnight. But these men were posted by that time.'

'And what were you waiting for then?' It amused Honeybath to reflect that throughout his late adventure within there had been platoons of policemen lurking without. 'A search warrant?'

'Mr Honeybath, one party had attempted to murder you. Hard upon that, and most irregularly, another party had whisked you away, nobody knew where. And when we *did* get to know where, we found an uncommonly odd set-up. This place passes as a gentleman's residence. It turns out to be a damned fortress.'

'Quite right, Mr Keybird. It's my own word for it. A fortress. Please go on.'

'We have had your safety to consider. I decided against precipitate action – and seem to have been justified in the event.'

'In fact, you waited until somebody more or less opened a door for you? Puzzling, that must have seemed.' Honeybath was now enjoying himself. 'A young fellow called Sinon, that was. Or I call him Sinon – you remember he turns up in the *Aeneid*. He's somewhere around now, arranging what he calls trip-wires. Or he may have dropped that, and be thinking up something else. There are only three other people here in the house, by the way – that, and an elderly man and a girl in a kind of annex. But Arbuthnot's lot will be arriving at any moment now to storm the place. It was for them that young Sinon opened the door. No doubt you can arrange to receive them in some suitable manner. Or arrange for some of your people to do so. If you take my advice, my dear Keybird, you'll address your own mind to something else.'

'To something else?' It was now agreeably evident that Detective Superintendent Keybird had been reduced to a state of stupefaction.

'Yes – because I'm sure that you want now to clear the whole matter up. You're a busy man, I know, and like to be done with things. Would you say that you have the major criminal trials of the last twenty years fairly well in your head?'

'Yes, I have.' Keybird's formerly alarming eyes were now fixed upon Honeybath in a kind of stony respect. 'Will you explain yourself, please?'

'By all means. But just cast your mind back for a moment to the 1950s. If possible, to October 1956. Would there have been any particularly notable criminal trial then?'

'Of course there was. William Mangrove, who carried out the biggest bullion robbery ever known in England.'

'Ah! Well, my dear chap, I think I may say that your William Mangrove is my Mr X.'

'Absolute nonsense!' If Keybird was outraged, he was startled as well. 'Mangrove – '

'*William* Mangrove. One always has to remember the brother – who founded, you'll recall, what may be termed the Chile branch of the family.'

'What the dickens do you know about those people?'

'Just take it that I've been investigating. Of course – although I don't myself actually see it that way – Mr X may be the brother from Valparaiso. It's always tricky with identical twins, wouldn't you agree? Fortunately, we have those fingerprints.'

'We have *what*?'

'Just another instance of the Honeybath service, my dear Keybird. Please step this way.'

But at this point it must be chronicled, if with reluctance, that Charles Honeybath (eminent portrait painter turned amateur sleuth) had had his day – or, rather, his night. By the time Keybird had glanced at the two photographs and asked half a dozen questions he was again very much in command of the proceedings. And of this the first token was the immediate plunging of the house into darkness and silence.

There wasn't a sound. There wasn't a sound to suggest that the three men supposed to be asleep upstairs had awakened and become conscious of anything amiss. Sinon (whose treacherous duty it had been to set some snare – at a stair-head, no doubt – which would hopefully break their necks) – Sinon (who *must* be alerted and alarmed) had presumably not ratted anew and warned them. Honeybath had a poor opinion of Sinon; he judged it probable that the wretched youth was merely cowering in a cupboard, or perhaps endeavouring like a rat to escape through the cellarage. As for the Mariners in their annex, they (and the respectable woman, if she lived 'in') seemed not to have been aroused either. Almost certainly, they couldn't simply have got away. Since just after midnight, it seemed, every possible escape route had been sealed off. The fortress had become a baited trap – to which the entrance was still Sinon's open door.

'I think you and I will make part of the outside reception committee,' Keybird murmured to Honeybath. 'Interesting to see your former friends arrive, wouldn't you say?' He could now be thought of as treating Honeybath RA as he would treat a colleague of a rank precisely equivalent to his own. 'It's possible, of course, that they just won't. Young Sinon didn't drop any hint that he had to give the green light?'

'Some signal that all was in order? No, he didn't. But I suppose it would be an obvious precaution.'

'Except that almost any kind of signal would carry a slight element of risk. We'll just move a little up the drive.'

It was a chilly night, but Honeybath's first thought was that it felt marvellous to be once more in open air. He realized that on several occasions he had been reckoning it quite improbable that he would ever experience anything of the kind again. The police, who in those bizarre moments of first encounter inside the house had appeared so comically obtrusive and uncatlike of tread, gave no hint of their presence without. Yet they were probably quite as numerous as they had been on the scene of the wretched Peach's capture. This was now an undeniably comforting thought.

Suddenly a train whistled in the night. The sound was quite far away, but it made Honeybath jump. For a moment it was almost as if the walls of Imlac House were raising themselves invisibly around him. He wondered whether he would ever again set eyes on Mr X –

let alone on Mr X's portrait. It was a weird thought that Imlac might be no more than a few miles off. Two fastnesses of robber barons at deadly enmity, no farther apart than that. It was a mediaeval notion. But then England was perhaps turning mediaeval again in certain ways...The whispering voice of Detective Superintendent Keybird broke into this philosophical reflection.

'The high road's about half a mile away. They won't risk bringing their cars nearer than that. We may catch a glimpse of lights as they park.' Keybird glanced at the illuminated dial of his watch. 'But I don't much like the look of it. They're late.'

'Unless some of them are creeping up the drive, or through the gardens, now.'

'*Look!*'

Far away – to Honeybath's eye it was farther than half a mile – first one and then a second beam of light had appeared, swerved slightly, gone out.

'That's them,' Keybird said aloud and confidently. 'There's been a hold-up of some sort, but in twenty minutes we'll be having a chat with them. Time for a pipe, if you ask me. I keep mine for occasions just like this.' He seemed to fumble in a pocket, and then to think better of it. 'But you never know,' he murmured, with a return to his former caution. 'They may just possibly have a scout in the grounds already. We'll just stay snug.'

They stayed snug – although snug was scarcely the word for it. Honeybath, who now felt uncommonly keyed up, nerved himself for a short but shivering vigil. Five enormous minutes went by. Then suddenly behind them there was a muffled report, an odd hiss in air, and high above their heads there hung briefly in the heavens a blazing red star.

'Damnation!' Keybird had leapt into the drive, was flashing a powerful torch, and at the same time blowing furiously on a whistle. He was for all the world – Honeybath inconsequently thought – like a French *gendarme*, hysterically endeavouring to control the traffic.

'We've underestimated your bloody Sinon, I'd say. That's his light – and it's not a green one. But here we are. Bundle in.'

As if magically, a car had appeared beside them. Its dipped headlights cast a hard merciless light on the drive in front of them, and it was itself bathed in the lights of a second and seemingly identical car immediately behind it. They were very powerful-looking cars. Honeybath found himself inside the first – and this point being instantly and alarmingly in display – before he had fully understood what was happening to him.

'Imlac House,' Keybird was saying – and with his old trick of speaking to empty air.

'Yes, sir.'

'Find it on your map. No distance from the railway-line, and on its south side.'

'Located, sir.'

'Then go there. And forget that book of rules. If you crack our skulls open, remember the wives and kids get the medals.' This remark (which Honeybath interpreted as a pleasantry prescriptive upon such constabulary occasions) appeared to afford Keybird no particular relief. When he sat back, he was swearing softly.

'But do you think,' Honeybath asked, 'that they're at all likely to go back there?'

'It's at least a possibility.' Keybird's voice was grim. 'They'll have been thinking of it as a secure base for a little time ahead still. No notion we've contacted you, for example. No notion they wouldn't be returning to it tonight with their prisoners or booty or whatever damned thing they were after in this house behind us. And their get-away set-up – the big emergency thing – will certainly be located there. Funds, and so on, waiting to be grabbed there too, likely enough. In and out of it in ten minutes will be their idea, if you ask me. Did you see anything that would serve as a runway?'

'I've told you I saw hardly anything at all. Do you mean –'

'Yes, of course. These fellows have rather a fancy for taking to the air nowadays. We'll see.' Keybird lowered his voice. 'If this nursemaid in front will just push along her bloody pram,' he added savagely.

This sudden evidence of a certain agitation in Keybird impressed Honeybath unfavourably. The car, and the supporting car behind it, were already travelling at what he judged a madman's pace, such as no eagerness to apprehend a bunch of crooks, however eminent, could by any means excuse. The tyres screamed at every bend. The nocturnal scene flew indistinguishably past as if gone molten under the heat of an atomic explosion. From time to time lights momentarily appeared ahead of them – only to slew violently aside as if brutally propelled into a ditch. Honeybath tried to tell himself that here was excitement at last. He found that he had abruptly lost his sense of time. It must be funk again. He recalled shamefacedly that he'd thought he'd got clear of funk.

'House straight ahead, sir,' the driver's voice said calmly. 'Do I – '

'Go on, man!' Keybird's tone suggested fury held on an uncertain leash. 'Drive right up to their damned front door.'

21

At least there was no difficulty in identifying the front door of Imlac House. It stood wide open, and light was blazing out of it. Indeed, the place was lit up in rather a big way; one might have supposed, if it hadn't been so extremely improbable, that Basil Arbuthnot and his associates were giving a large party. Only one wing lay in darkness, and from its windows Honeybath was momentarily aware of a dull reddish glow. The night was over, he told himself, and here was the first reflected glint of sunrise. But this effect vanished as first the second and then a third police car drove up beside them, and the whole mansion became saturated in their headlights.

Keybird had tumbled out of the car, and Honeybath – still very aware of his bruises – scrambled after him. The final stretch of the drive was a scattering of policemen, all baring for the house. Honeybath ran with the rest, although he felt quite certain that the assault was too late. Arbuthnot and whatever confederates he had would by now have grabbed what they required, and departed. But now, and even as this conviction came to him, there appeared, silhouetted in the front door, the figure of a woman carrying a suitcase. She paused irresolutely, and then ran down the steps and along the front of the house. It wasn't a very bright proceeding on this last straggler's part. But she had a fair start on the nearest constable, and was still uncaptured as she vanished round a corner of the building. Her momentary appearance had served one purpose. Honeybath now knew that here was the seat of his late adventures, without possibility of mistake. For the woman had been Sister Agnes.

The entire body of police were now following her – this at some shouted command from Keybird himself. And in a moment Honeybath knew why. From somewhere behind the house – which was perhaps the side on which the park lay – there had come the splutter and roar of an engine starting into life. It wasn't the engine of a motor car. Honeybath recalled Keybird's saying that big-time crooks of Arbuthnot's sort had a fancy nowadays for taking to the air.

Honeybath found himself, rather to his surprise, in the van of the pursuers. He recalled, in a confused way and as if out of somebody else's biography, that he had been a faster sprinter than the future PM at that private school. But ahead of any of them was now a vehicle: a multi-wheeled affair of a paramilitary sort which the police had somehow conjured out of thin air. This had what might be called a young searchlight mounted on its roof; the beam from it swung wildly about as the vehicle recklessly charged down a flight of steps from a terrace and over what appeared to be a rockery. It slowed abruptly, and came to a halt. When the searchlight steadied, what it picked out was a helicopter.

To charge down a helicopter about to rise in air would appear to be a feat of some difficulty. The running policemen did for a moment hesitate, and it looked much as if their bag would consist of Sister Agnes alone. For the door of the helicopter had been shut, and for the abandoned woman – now insensately yelling at it – it showed no disposition to open again. The engine roared and spluttered, roared once more and again spluttered rather badly. At this point the paramilitary vehicle (not, Honeybath thought, at Keybird's command, but simply as developing a mind of its own) charged forward again like a bull at a matador. For this particular matador the only evasive action possible was on a perpendicular dimension. And, sure enough, as the bull hurtled forward the matador rose in air. The motion had every appearance of triumphant power. The helicopter, in fact, had vanished into the heavens with all the confidence of a briskly levitating saint.

The pursuing vehicle screamed and jerked to a halt, baffled. Its searchlight swung upward on an arc, and for a moment searched the skies in vain. Then it found the helicopter, and held it – a fast diminishing object, soaring into the pale-grey dawn. The roar of its engine grew fainter. The roar of the engine abruptly stopped; there was a brief splutter again; the helicopter vanished from within its halo of light. A moment later, and from ground-level, came a crash, a shattering explosion, a leaping sheet of flame. And within the same fraction of a second it was just possible to distinguish another and totally different sound. In itself this sound would normally have been quite something, since it represented the shattering of every pane of glass on the vulnerable side of Imlac House.

Finally, there was Detective Superintendent Keybird's voice. It spoke close to Honeybath's ear, but might have been a dwarf's.

'Poor bastards,' Keybird said. 'No time to warm up their bloody bus.'

From this appalling spectacle Honeybath turned away – literally and through an angle of 180 degrees. The result was not exactly relaxing. Imlac House was on fire too.

And it was quite an independent affair. For a moment, indeed, it was natural to suppose that the one disaster was a consequence of the other; that incendiary material from the helicopter had somehow transmitted itself to the building. But this was impossible. The helicopter's fate had overtaken it only seconds ago. Imlac was already well alight. Honeybath remembered the dull glow he had remarked in the windows of one wing. That had been the start of what he was witnessing now. The gang, in fact, had fired their stronghold as they left it. It was an awesome thought. To kindle one conflagration and be destroyed by another almost at once was as macabre a feat as could be conceived.

But for what rational purpose had Arbuthnot and his crew paused to effect the immolation of Imlac? The answer was clear. They had been determined to leave as few intelligible traces of themselves as possible. And the best means of securing that end had been indiscriminate destruction. There would be things impossible to carry away in a hurry which might yet –

Charles Honeybath found that he was running again.

So, whether in one direction or another, were most of the policemen. They were being required, he supposed, to turn themselves into impromptu firemen as best they could until the real Fire Brigade arrived. It was as a consequence of this necessity, no doubt, that his immediate conduct went unremarked.

There could be little chance of the fire's not rapidly spreading through the entire extent of Imlac. It had been started with calculated skill at the windward end of the house, and dawn was bringing with it a freshening breeze which must already be assisting the flames on their way. But what emerged from the central block at present was mostly smoke. Rather a lot of smoke, it was true. But smoke incinerates nobody, and you can probably make a dash through quite a wall of it, if only you treat it as a diver treats water. Or so Honeybath speculated, and decided that the speculation was to be acted upon.

Unfortunately he had to waste time in getting round to the farther side of the house. That open front door, glimpsed as he had been driven up, represented his only notion of how to get inside. On the other hand there was just a chance that by entering that way he would find himself on not totally unfamiliar ground. He did have a dim memory of a large hall, and also a curiously sharp visual impression of that lift and its immediate surroundings. And the lift, could he gain it and operate it, would take him to territory his knowledge of which was not in doubt.

He rounded a corner, gained a terrace, and raced along it with the main façade of the mansion on his right hand. Somebody shouted at him – warningly, he supposed – but from quite far off; there wasn't a chance that he could be intercepted now. Electric lighting was still on all over the place, and as he dashed up a short flight of steps and through the front door he was for seconds more conscious of being blinded by the glare than suffocated by the smoke. In fact there wasn't much smoke – not here as yet. And in another second – quite wonderfully – the lift was before him. He pressed a button, and its door opened; he entered, pressed another button, and the door closed and he began to ascend. It was as easy as that. He felt ashamed of being disposed to import a certain element of bravado into so little hazardous an operation. He would be out again within ten minutes. And with him would be the portrait of Mr X – if, that was to say, the scoundrels had abandoned it to the flames. He didn't now kid himself that they were likely to have done anything else.

Nor had they. What he thought of as his own corridor was brightly illuminated; so was his painting-room through its open door; and there his canvas was, negligently perched against a wall. He grabbed it, turned, and ran. He found himself running towards a sheet of flame.

And he was running amid uproar. He recalled from the era of the blitz how nothing is more terrifying about a large blaze than the sheer racket and crackle of it. You used to imagine that paratroops had descended and that there was small-arms fire going on all around you. But at least he had regained the door of the lift, although the hot breath of the monster was now on his brow.

And then he remembered the Monet.

It would have been silly to pretend that going on to his bedroom was other than the act of a lunatic. But no – it could in a fashion be rationalized. For some weird reason this seemed important to Honeybath as he plunged on. There would still be towels, running water. You soaked something and wrapped it round you…that sort of thing. But, in fact, a Monet was a Monet (which didn't mean it was a Cézanne). And a Honeybath was just a Honeybath. He'd rescue both, but he wouldn't just rescue his own damned masterpiece alone. Perhaps it was equally rational simply to stand by the way you were made. The way God had secretly made you – deep inside Honeybath, successful RA.

For the inside of a couple of minutes more God seemed to be approving of this romantically disinterested performance. Honeybath was conscious of a singeing smell, and suspected it came from his own hair. But he had a picture under each arm, and the lift was yet again before him. Then God switched off. It was almost literally like that. All the lights went out. Presumably the Fire Brigade had arrived – or the police had remembered the first thing the Fire Brigade does: cut off the power-supply at its source.

Not in complete darkness, but to a lurid flicker, Honeybath pressed the button. Not unnaturally, nothing happened. And he wondered where, in this damned house, the staircases lay.

He was lying on grass, bathed in the hard light of arc lamps. He heard the crash of a falling roof, and then the voice of Detective Superintendent Keybird. Keybird, in one of his furies, was yelling something about his being a bloody fool. He recalled the mildly comical fact that 'bloody' was the strongest swear-word this top cop allowed himself. Keybird was pointing.

'What the hell is that?' Keybird yelled.

'It's the *Portrait of an Unknown Gentleman.*'

'And *that*?'

Honeybath rolled over and glimpsed Claude Monet's *Water Lilies*. Just one among industrious old Monet's innumerable expanses of the things.

'*Il miglior fabbro,*' Charles Honeybath said, and fainted away.

22

It was a very good breakfast – or very good for a casually chosen country pub. Honeybath was doing justice to it; he found himself much more hungry than tired. But Keybird was letting his coffee (and even the coffee wasn't bad) grow cold. The files which had arrived (in a more dependable helicopter) from New Scotland Yard were absorbing him completely. But eventually he looked up.

'You began from the portrait,' he said.

'Yes, of course. After all, I'd painted it.'

'It strikes me, if I may say so, as pretty good. Not that I'm an expert, Mr Honeybath.'

'It's not painted for experts. It's painted for posterity – just like the Monet.'

'Yes, of course. I understand the feeling. But you began from it right at the start?'

'I think I may be said to have begun from *The Red-Headed League*.'

'From *what*?'

'One of the earliest of the Sherlock Holmes stories. I can recall it perfectly clearly, although I haven't read it for forty years. Jabez Somebody is a pawnbroker with red hair. He's lured away from his shop for a considerable period of time in order to sit somewhere or other copying out the *Encyclopaedia Britannica* for quite good pay. He's been told a fantastic story about an American millionaire who has left money to benefit red-headed men in this absurd way. It was really because a band of crooks wanted to operate from his cellar – 'running a tunnel to some other building'. I believe these are dear old

Conan Doyle's *ipsissima verba*. Well, I just saw that I was not a Jabez. The proportions of the whole thing simply didn't admit of the bank robbery's being the main thing. It was a sideline – as we now know.'

'We do, indeed.'

'Unlike the handwritten *Encyclopaedia*, the portrait of Mr X was really *needed*. But *why*? Well, a portrait by me – to say nothing of accompanying sketches with the sitter's thumbprints on them – is evidence of the sitter's being alive. But there are less oblique, laborious, and expensive ways of proving a man alive. You can just exhibit him. But it wouldn't be easy to exhibit Mr X – William Mangrove, that is – convincingly without exhibiting something else as well: Mr X's hopeless imbecility and pervasive amnesia. "We've *got* Mangrove. Pay up, or we use the information he can provide us with." That, roughly speaking, was the formula I seemed to see.'

'Mr Honeybath, you're wasted as a portrait painter. If you'd taken to another line of business, you'd have beaten Dupin, Holmes – the whole lot.' Keybird had produced this outrageous sentiment on a note of unflawed admiration. 'For how right you were.'

'But my understanding of the affair – the role of the twin brother, for example – stops just there.' Honeybath pointed to the files. 'And, if it isn't too irregular, I'd like to *know*.'

'Regularity be damned,' Keybird said. 'Listen.'

'Things were a bit primitive back in the fifties,' Keybird began in a reminiscent tone. 'There was only a single really big gang – the one run by William and Henry Mangrove. It was formidable enough, largely because they were men of education and had several of their own sort around them. But the Great Bullion Robbery broke them. At least, it seemed like that. William was gaoled for a long term of years, and Henry bolted abroad and was never heard of again. Not that there wasn't a fly in the ointment. The bullion was never recovered.'

'Not a scrap of it?'

'Not a scrap. And we only knew two things. The first was that there were enough villains living in unobtrusive affluence to show that a certain amount of it had been successfully marketed. The other was that the original Mangrove gang had split in half. And both halves prospered. Where there had been one big criminal organization there were now two.' Keybird chuckled. 'And you've passed the time of day with both of them.'

'Quite so.'

'We'll give these two rival gangs your own names: the Arbuthnot gang and the Mariner gang. Well, the next publicly known facts are these: William Mangrove escaped from gaol and vanished. His charred remains were recovered from a burnt-out house in Manchester some weeks later.'

'But they weren't really his remains at all.'

'Obviously they were his brother's. Now, what seems to have happened was this. The Mariner gang controlled by far the greater part of the booty, and they became nervous that William Mangrove, locked up in gaol as he was, was going to be got at in some way and persuaded to talk. So they decided to spring him.'

'To what?'

'To effect his escape – which they did. But villains sprung in that way are never very good lives. As often as not, they're got out only to be effectively silenced for good. Murdered, in fact.'

'Good God!'

'As you say – good God.' Keybird was faintly amused. 'But the Mariner gang reckoned without the extreme cunning of the Arbuthnot gang. Henry Mangrove was back in England by this time, and the Arbuthnot gang contrived to switch brothers at what might be called just the psychological moment. So when the Mariner gang thought they were liquidating William they were in fact liquidating Henry. And, of course, the Arbuthnot gang had got William. He looked like being an immensely powerful weapon in the bitter struggle in which the rival gangs were by this time engaged. Only, of course, here's something psychological again.' Keybird grinned. 'William Mangrove turned out to believe himself to be the Emperor Napoleon. And he remembered nothing that could be of either the slightest use or harm to anybody. It became the tactic of the

Arbuthnot gang to prove they held the authentic William Mangrove while concealing this awkward mental deficiency. And that's where your portrait came in.'

'A damned expensive dodge, if you ask me. And they paid me the whole fee! I can't get over that.'

'Vanity. Impossible to overestimate the vanity of those cattle. And they really *did* want a slap-up portrait of their former admired chief. For their boardroom, no doubt. Aping their betters.' Keybird paused. 'If they *are* much their betters,' he added cynically. 'Big business and big crime – you can have the lot, so far as I'm concerned.'

'It's a point of view.' Honeybath was a little startled by this heterodox flash from a pillar of the law. 'But what then?'

'When the Arbuthnot lot discovered that the Mariner girl had contacted you they promptly tried to kill you instantly. Failing at that, and knowing the Mariners had carried you off, they realized that their whole plan was a frost, since your account of your adventures would reveal the complete uselessness of poor old Mr X. So they mounted what may he called a counter-offensive in a great hurry – contacting the treacherous Sinon and arranging their raid.'

'What good was it going to do them?'

'They were going to carry off Mariner as a hostage, I suppose. And, no doubt, deal with you more effectively, second time round. You knew too much.'

'Well, well, well.' Honeybath made to pour himself another cup of coffee, and then paused. 'They took William Mangrove on the helicopter with them?'

'Yes, they did. I suppose they didn't like to think of such an eminent old wreck being returned inside. A humanitarian thought, you might say.'

'Everybody in it died instantly?'

'Everybody. Six men, all told.'

'Able was I ere I saw Elba.'

'I beg your pardon?' Keybird was puzzled.

'Oh, nothing. Just something Mr X once said.' Honeybath's glance went to his portrait, which stood against the wall of the pub's little coffee-room. 'I suppose my painting will have to be produced in evidence?'

'Definitely, I'd say. The Mariners, so called, will be going on trial. And Crumble and Sister Agnes and several others.'

'I don't like the idea of it.'

'Of these people getting their deserts?' Keybird was astonished.

'Not that. And I shan't mind figuring at the Old Bailey. Only, I'd rather my painting didn't.'

'Now, that's a very odd thing.' And Keybird shook his head uncomprehendingly. 'I'd suppose it to be a very good advertisement, Mr Honeybath. A very good advertisement, indeed.'

MICHAEL INNES

APPLEBY AT ALLINGTON

Sir John Appleby dines one evening at Allington Park, the Georgian home of his acquaintance, Owain Allington, who is new to the area. His curiosity is aroused when Allington mentions his nephew and heir to the estate, Martin Allington, whose name Appleby recognises. The evening comes to an end but, just as Appleby is leaving, they find a dead man – electrocuted in the *son et lumière* box that had been installed in the grounds.

APPLEBY ON ARARAT

Inspector Appleby is stranded on a very strange island, with a rather odd bunch of people – too many men, too few women (and one of them too attractive) cause a deal of trouble. But that is nothing compared to later developments, including the body afloat in the water and the attack by local inhabitants.

'Every sentence he writes has flavour, every incident flamboyance'
– *The Times Literary Supplement*

MICHAEL INNES

THE DAFFODIL AFFAIR

Inspector Appleby's aunt is most distressed when her horse, Daffodil – a somewhat half-witted animal with exceptional numerical skills – goes missing from her stable in Harrogate. Meanwhile, Hudspith is hot on the trail of Lucy Rideout, an enigmatic young girl who has been whisked away to an unknown isle by a mysterious gentleman. And when a house in Bloomsbury, supposedly haunted, also goes missing, the baffled policemen search for a connection. As Appleby and Hudspith trace Daffodil and Lucy, the fragments begin to come together and an extravagant project is uncovered, leading them to a South American jungle.

'Yet another surprising firework display of wit and erudition and ingenious invention' – *The Guardian*

DEATH AT THE PRESIDENT'S LODGING

Inspector Appleby is called to St Anthony's College, where the President has been murdered in his Lodging. Scandal abounds when it becomes clear that the only people with any motive to murder him are the only people who had the opportunity – because the President's Lodging opens off Orchard Ground, which is locked at night, and only the Fellows of the College have keys…

'It is quite the most accomplished first crime novel that I have read…all first-rate entertainment'
– Cecil Day Lewis, *The Daily Telegraph*

MICHAEL INNES

HAMLET, REVENGE!

At Seamnum Court, seat of the Duke of Horton, The Lord Chancellor of England is murdered at the climax of a private presentation of *Hamlet*, in which he plays Polonius. Inspector Appleby pursues some of the most famous names in the country, unearthing dreadful suspicion.

'Michael Innes is in a class by himself among writers of detective fiction' – *The Times Literary Supplement*

THE LONG FAREWELL

Lewis Packford, the great Shakespearean scholar, was thought to have discovered a book annotated by the Bard – but there is no trace of this valuable object when Packford apparently commits suicide. Sir John Appleby finds a mixed bag of suspects at the dead man's house, who might all have a good motive for murder. The scholars and bibliophiles who were present might have been tempted by the precious document in Packford's possession. And Appleby discovers that Packford had two secret marriages, and that both of these women were at the house at the time of his death.

TITLES BY MICHAEL INNES AVAILABLE DIRECT
FROM HOUSE OF STRATUS

Quantity		£	$(US)	€
	THE AMPERSAND PAPERS	6.99	9.95	13.50
	APPLEBY AND HONEYBATH	6.99	9.95	13.50
	APPLEBY AND THE OSPREYS	6.99	9.95	13.50
	APPLEBY AT ALLINGTON	6.99	9.95	13.50
	THE APPLEBY FILE	6.99	9.95	13.50
	APPLEBY ON ARARAT	6.99	9.95	13.50
	APPLEBY PLAYS CHICKEN	6.99	9.95	13.50
	APPLEBY TALKING	6.99	9.95	13.50
	APPLEBY TALKS AGAIN	6.99	9.95	13.50
	APPLEBY'S ANSWER	6.99	9.95	13.50
	APPLEBY'S END	6.99	9.95	13.50
	APPLEBY'S OTHER STORY	6.99	9.95	13.50
	AN AWKWARD LIE	6.99	9.95	13.50
	THE BLOODY WOOD	6.99	9.95	13.50
	CARSON'S CONSPIRACY	6.99	9.95	13.50
	A CHANGE OF HEIR	6.99	9.95	13.50
	CHRISTMAS AT CANDLESHOE	6.99	9.95	13.50
	A CONNOISSEUR'S CASE	6.99	9.95	13.50
	THE DAFFODIL AFFAIR	6.99	9.95	13.50
	DEATH AT THE CHASE	6.99	9.95	13.50
	DEATH AT THE PRESIDENT'S LODGING	6.99	9.95	13.50
	A FAMILY AFFAIR	6.99	9.95	13.50
	FROM LONDON FAR	6.99	9.95	13.50
	THE GAY PHOENIX	6.99	9.95	13.50

ALL HOUSE OF STRATUS BOOKS ARE AVAILABLE FROM GOOD BOOKSHOPS
OR DIRECT FROM THE PUBLISHER:

Internet: www.houseofstratus.com including synopses and features.

Email: sales@houseofstratus.com
info@houseofstratus.com
(please quote author, title and credit card details.)